TROUBLE DOWN THE TUNNEL

PESHA

First published by Pibly 2012

ISBN-13: 978-0-9538620-1-6

DEDICATION

To the memory of my loving parents.

To all my wonderful family and friends.

CONTENTS

ACKNOWLEDGEMENTS

To those known and unknown who have prayed for me.

To all the unknown people on the Internet who added to my knowledge.

To those I have met through life who have given me inspiration.

To Hal Ackerman for his helpful ideas.

To God be the Glory - Oft times in tremendous frustration I would pray what I called my Bezaleel prayer where I would tell God He gave Bezaleel wisdom and understanding to know how to work all manner of works for the service of the sanctuary. (Exodus 36.1) My prayers were repeatedly answered.

CHAPTER ONE

Struggling through the thick undergrowth Harry and Pete were sweating profusely. Their eyes were wide with fear.

Their smart city suits were torn and stained from the rich foliage. With a deep sense of foreboding they realised without a miracle they would be caught.

The old Mercedes careered down the road. Mark Appleyard gripped the steering wheel tightly. He had a steadfast, determined look on his face. In his heart he had no care for anyone or anything.

As if it had a mind of its own, the car bounced from kerb to kerb with an almost sideward trajectory. The steering wheel shuddered in Mark's hands. There was a smell of burning from the tyres. He narrowly missed oncoming cars which perilously swerved out of his way.

The ride became ever more fraught as they entered country roads. Mark had no respect for the narrow roads or their endless bends. He had a total disregard he could not see round these corners. More importantly he was heedless as to the safety and welfare of his passengers.

His bright blue eyes were aflame with fury. He kept clenching and unclenching his hands making his driving even more perilous.

Next to him, his wife, Madge, clasped her hands to her face in fear.

"Stop it! Stop it! You'll get us all killed," Madge yelled. "You're mad."

Mark continued to stare ahead as though he were in a trance. He totally ignored the pleadings of his wife.

A low bridge jumped out at them. Mark swerved and narrowly missed its side structure.

"Mark, stop, stop the car. What do you think you're playing at?" screamed Madge. Her face scrunched up with fear.

"Shut up, woman," was Mark's tight lipped reply.

Their eight year old son, Andy, held onto the seat in front for grim life. He gripped so tightly, his hands had pain shooting down them. His heart was full of fear. Was this his wonderful Dad doing this?

"Dad, please stop the car. I'll be a good boy." Andy sobbed.

Mark ignored him and jammed the accelerator down harder. He drove the car even faster and more recklessly. As they skidded round a corner Andy wretched and screamed out

"Daaaad, I'm going to be sick." Mark swerved into the kerb and slammed on the brakes.

Andy stumbled out of the car and was sick all over the verge.

Madge hurried to Andy's side. She put her arms round him and comforted him.

Her predicament was immense.

They were in a small country lane miles from anywhere. If she stayed out of the car, she wondered when the next car would come along and help them. If they went back in the car, how would Mark drive. She kept weighing up the position.

Andy ran up to his Dad and hugged him.

"Dad, I really will be a good boy."

Mark looked down at his son. He blinked a few times as if trying to focus his mind. He looked at Andy with almost a vacant expression on his face.

"Get into the car, now."

Before Madge could stop him Andy ran obediently and sat in the back of the car quivering.

Madge looked into Mark's eyes in bewilderment. Her blood ran cold with what she saw there: anger and hatred were intermingled.

She knew she had no choice. She reluctantly got back into the car.

She hoped Mark would be more responsible after what he had done to his son.

The ride home was slower but silent. Andy tried to be very silent. He clenched his arms to his body to try and suppress the sobs and tears which bubbled up inside him. Occasionally, a muffled sob escaped.

Madge knew deep within her heart they could not go on like this.

When they arrived home in Chorley, Madge grabbed Andy out of the car and rushed into the house. Mark parked the car in the garage and stormed into their home.

The arguments started. A screaming match ensued. Andy watched shivering and open mouthed.

"You must be crazy to drive like that," Madge said accusingly.

"Oh shut up, woman. I didn't want to waste my life driving leisurely along country lanes."

"Waste your life? You nearly cost us ours. Don't you ever think of anyone but yourself?"

"That's the trouble with you; you always drivel on, blah, blah, blah." He angrily retorted.

"I wish I'd never married you. I don't know what's got into you," said Madge.

"It isn't me who is the problem it's you." Mark's eyes were bulging with anger.

"You don't know what the problem is? You've nearly killed us all. I think you need to see a psychiatrist. You've never been right since you started work at that factory."

Back and forth the taunts and accusations raged, each one becoming more vicious than the last.

Madge's head was full of confusion and shock. Here was the man she deeply loved all these years acting like a lunatic. One minute he was the old, adorable, lovable Mark. The next he was irritable which descended into downright horrid. He switched from saying beautiful loving things to tirades of abuse. He was caring in practical details of their life, and then changed into this irrational monster.

The argument became more and more heated. Andy could bear it no longer. He ran and put on his headphones to cut out the noise. He curled up embryonic fashion with a book. His mind was in a whirl. What was happening to his Mum and Dad whom he loved so much?

Reading his novel was out of the question. There was no way he could concentrate with all this shouting and bawling going on.

He listened and watched as the adults ranted and raved at each other. He wondered what he had done wrong for all this to happen.

When his Dad hit his Mum, Andy shot up from where he was sitting. His book fell to the floor. He ran at his Dad. He pummelled him with his fists as hard as he could.

"Don't hit my Mum. Don't hit my Mum. I hate you, I hate you, I hate you." How could the Dad he loved so much do this to his Mum?

"That's the last straw," Madge screamed, "I'm leaving you and taking Andy with me."

Madge flounced out of the room. She stumbled on the steps as she rushed upstairs.

Hurriedly, she packed. She flung open the wardrobe and pulled out a brown suitcase which had wheels attached. She threw in shoes, clothes - coat hangers and all, into the suitcase. She scooped up a load of underwear and smaller garments from a chest of drawer and threw them into the suitcase. She collected toiletries for her and Andy.

Mark followed her. He sobbed.

"I love you. Don't leave me."

He tried to put his arm round her. She glared at him and violently pushed him away. She ignored him as he followed her. She went from room to room collecting items to take with her.

Mark went into every room with her, protesting he loved her.

"Don't leave me, don't leave me," he kept saying.

Madge totally ignored him and continued packing. She shouted through to Andy.

"Get your rucksack? Put anything you especially want in it."

Barely half an hour went by and she was ready to leave.

She called a taxi. In a few minutes the taxi drew up at the door. Madge shouted to Andy.

"Hurry up the taxi is here."

They quickly walked down the pathway. Andy kept glancing back at his Dad. His mind and heart were in turmoil. He could hear Mark still saying.

"Don't leave me. I love you both."

Mark watched in bewilderment as the taxi drove out of view. He could not understand why they were having all these rows nowadays. He put his head into his hands and sobbed.

Madge asked the taxi driver about accommodation. He told her of a local estate agent and drove her there.

Within the hour, she and Andy were settled in rented accommodation. Thankfully, it was within walking distance of Andy's school. It was comfortable but rather expensive. Madge wondered how she was going to manage.

CHAPTER TWO

The blades of the chopper whirled overhead. There was a sudden blast of gunfire. Harry let out a smothered squeal. Blood poured from his right arm.

"Andy, Andy," his Mother called anxiously, "come and eat your breakfast."

"Oh Mum," he shouted back, "I was getting to the exciting bit in my book."

"Never mind about that," her voice unusually curt, "breakfast is ready and we're going to stay at Auntie Mary's during the school holidays."

Andy heaved a huge sigh.

"Oh, no, not again, everything at her house is so very boring. I hate it there. There's nothing to do and nothing ever happens."

"You read too many thrillers." Although, to tell you the truth, she was relieved he did so much reading. It helped to take his mind away from what was happening.

He ate his breakfast as slowly as he could. He hoped they would miss the bus to his Auntie's house.

"Hurry up, Andy," his Mum said, somewhat exasperatedly, "I've packed your bags. Go and collect them from the lounge."

As Andy went into the lounge, she called after him with a hint of laugher in her voice.

"Don't forget to bring your latest thriller with you."

They were going through the front door when the telephone rang. Dropping the bags she was holding, his Mum ran back into the lounge. She was very annoyed anyone rang when they were in such a big hurry.

"Why do people always ring when you're going out?"

Andy strained to listen but was unable to tell who was on the line. His Mum sounded very agitated.

All his Mum seemed to say was "yes, no."

His ears pricked up when he heard her say, "Andy." After, he heard nothing as she lowered her voice considerably. After a few minutes she appeared to slam the receiver down on the other person.

"Who was that?" asked Andy as his Mother came back.

"No-one important," she tried to sound offhand. If Andy were more observant he would have noticed how flushed her face was.

They gathered up their cases. Andy slung his rucksack on his back and they set off down the Avenue. Andy dawdled as much as he dare.

"Oh, hurry up Andy, or we'll miss the bus."

"But.."

"No, but, just hurry up."

After a while, Andy asked.

"What about Dad? Won't he wonder where we are?"

A curious look shot across his Mum's face. She did not want to tell Andy it was his Dad on the phone.

"Oh, he'll be alright." She answered somewhat brusquely.

Andy knew his Mum well enough when he could push her further and this was not the moment.

"He knows we're going to Auntie Mary's," she added.

At the reminder of Auntie Mary's name, Andy pulled a face.

"Who else would live in such a small village where the bus only came once a day?" He thought.

A slow, crafty smile slowly moved across his face as he thought of finding a large hedgehog and putting it in his cousin's bed when she came to stay. He would love to have put it in Auntie Mary's bed but even he knew that was a step too far.

Gloom soon returned to him as they arrived at the bus stop. They waited ten minutes as Madge was always early. His heart dropped when he saw the red number 162 bus speeding towards them.

The conductor helped Madge drag the wheeled suitcase onto the bus.

Paying was a bit difficult as Madge had so many bags to juggle. They flopped into a seat.

After they travelled for about half an hour, Madge produced some sandwiches. Andy slowly opened the wrappers. He played with the wrappers of the sandwich.

"Who's going to help me with my model aeroplanes if Dad can't?"

"Eat up your sandwiches," Madge replied.

"Do we have to go to Auntie Mary's? She's such an old Dragon. It's so boring. Nothing ever happens."

"Don't talk about your Auntie like that. Just eat up your sandwiches."

Petulantly, Andy threw his sandwich on his Mother's suitcase. Madge pretended not to notice. The last thing she wanted was a big row on the bus.

Andy turned his attention to looking round the bus. At least the bus had a window where you could turn a dial on it and it let in fresh air. He desperately wanted his tousled blond hair to get in a mess. He had already scuffed his best black shoes on the pavement whilst they waited for the bus. His Mum had not noticed…yet. Nor had she noticed he had changed back into his comfortable old trousers and shirt for they were hidden by his new fawn raincoat.

Why was it when you went to Auntie Mary's you must look your best? Surely, she was a little girl once? Mind you, it was such a long time ago she would never remember.

Christmas and birthdays were a nightmare as he had to write so carefully when he thanked her. If his Mum were disappointed with his effort, he had to start again.

All his letters must begin with, "Dear Auntie Mary, How are you? I hope you are very well. Thank you very much for the lovely present you sent me."

Best clothes for Auntie Mary, write to Auntie Mary, thank Auntie Mary. Yes Mummy, no Mummy, my big toe Mummy.

His Mother seemed pre-occupied with other matters on the journey. Her face kept puckering in sadness as she thought of all the recent weeks and the huge decision she made to leave Mark. Deep down, she really loved Mark. But she dare not risk her and Andy's future and welfare with a maniac.

Andy read the weekly comic he brought with him. Somewhat nonchalantly, he stretched out his hand for the sandwich where he threw it. He loved his Mother's salad sandwiches.

Eventually, they passed the village Church. Andy knew it was only a few minutes more before they arrived in Auntie Mary's village.

They alighted from the bus on the deserted main road in the picturesque village. They walked a mile deeper into the countryside. Madge dragged the wheeled suitcase. She managed to carry the other bags astride the suitcase. It made it a lot easier except when she was negotiating kerbs, when the other bags slipped and slid to one side. She grabbed them quickly to prevent them falling off.

Andy walked a few feet behind with his head bowed and his hands in his pockets. Thankfully, it was a sunny day but there was no sunshine in Andy's heart.

They turned into an avenue lined with trees. Andy let out a big sigh as his Auntie's house came into view.

A large, rambling, detached house set in an acre of wilderness. They made their way round to the rear of the house. Andy was not interested in the pretty pink climbing rose which made an arch over the back door. He would have preferred to slither through the undergrowth like Pete and Harry.

Now we have the kissing part, he said to himself. His Auntie, a well built matronly woman, came bustling out to meet them. Her dark hair was tied severely back in a bun. Her functional apron covered what might have been a modern dress forty years earlier.

Her podgy arms seemed to envelop him. He could hardly come up for air as she gave him a big kiss. He quickly wiped it off his face. After all, he was eight now. It was all very soppy and was for girls.

"My, Andy, how you've grown."

It was always the same. How you've grown? How is school? Which class are you in now? She did not pause for replies nor did she seem to come up for air. He could recite it before she spoke. However, he liked the next bit.

"Andy, I've some of my home-made cake for you."

Somehow, Auntie Mary's cake tasted like no-one else's. It was a light sponge cake filled with jam with a light sprinkling of icing sugar on top. She made her jam from the raspberries she grew in her garden.

Whilst Andy enjoyed his cake in the kitchen, he saw his Mother and Auntie talking. They kept their voices very low.

He heard only snippets. He saw his Auntie hand his Mum an envelope which she opened. She studied the letter and tore it up. She thrust the pieces in her pocket.

The telephone rang. Auntie Mary answered it. She handed the phone to Madge. Madge twirled her hair as she answered with a few "yes's."

Madge slammed the phone down.

"Was that Dad?" asked Andy.

"I think it's time you went out to play," replied Auntie Mary.

With a piqued look, Andy ran into the garden. His arms whirled aeroplane fashion. He dreamed of the day he could fly a plane or a helicopter and look for criminals hiding in the undergrowth.

Suddenly, there was a rustle in the undergrowth. Andy started. He felt the hairs on the back of his neck prickling like mad.

"You silly thing," he said to himself, "it's only a bird."

Another rustle, a branch of the Birch tree, with its distinctive bark and beautiful leaves, moved slightly. Two dark eyes peered at him.

Andy was in confusion. Should he to run as fast as he could back to the house or investigate further?

Very nervously, he edged forward, bit by bit. As he got nearer he saw the bottom of a dress.

"Oh, it's only a girl," was his reaction.

"Come out of there," he said, in the firmest, deepest voice he could muster, "come out of there, at once." He was not going to be beaten by a mere slip of a girl.

Slowly, a bedraggled, thin girl with dark, long hair emerged. She looked very bohemian with a multi-coloured dress on: primarily it was bright red and yellow. The bottom was a bit torn. Her trainers were scratched and dirty.

She looked at Andy with her big brown eyes which penetrated right through him. She moved as if she would run away.

"Stop!" Andy shouted out, "or I'll tell the Police." At the same time, he lurched forward and grabbed her arm.

Letting out a squeal, she pulled and pushed Andy with all her strength. Now, it was his turn to yelp as she sunk her strong teeth into his arm.

By now, he was determined to find out who she was. He held on grimly but with great difficulty. His right arm was throbbing like mad.

They struggled and struggled. They fell to the grassy floor. They wrestled and rolled over and over. Andy managed to hold her with one of her arms up her back. She went limp.

Roughly, he pulled her to her feet. He looked her full in the face.

"What are you doing here? What's your name? Where've you come from?" The questions poured out of his mouth.

"I, I, I, "she stammered and began to cry.

"Aren't girls soppy?" thought Andy. "They're such cry babies."

Without thinking, he weakened his grasp. With a sharp tug, she was away through the undergrowth. Andy pursued her. The branches smashed back into his face. He stopped. There was silence.

"Now which way has she gone?" He had no clues. He messed around for about half an hour searching for her but to no avail. It were as if she had fallen down a rabbit hole.

CHAPTER THREE

Pete's wrists smarted from the tight handcuffs. He looked toward Harry who had a huge white bandage on his arm. Roughly, the Police Officer took them into the Courtroom. Pete knew no-one would believe their incredible story.

There was a slight noise in Andy's bedroom. Andy looked up from his exciting book. His Mother stood in the doorway.

She was tall, slim, with long, dark wavy hair. Her smart, brown, designer label suit was beautiful. Only she knew she found it in a local Charity shop.

Unusually, her face was very serious. Andy detected a slight smudge of her make-up round her eyes.

"Mum, where're we going?" His heart leaped with joyful anticipation. Perhaps they were going home early. Already they had been at Auntie Mary's a whole day. Apart from his skirmish with that girl, the hours had passed very, very slowly.

"No, Andy, I've to go by myself."

Seeing his quizzical look, "I've to go to Manchester on business."

"Oh, Mum, can't I come? Please, please," he weakly added.

"No, you've to spend the day with Auntie Mary."

You could feel the instant gloominess descend on Andy.

She was sorry to see his crestfallen look.

"Cheer up, Andy, I'll bring a present back for you."

"It wasn't much compensation, but it was better than nothing," thought Andy.

In her hand he saw some rolled up papers. They looked rather official.

"What are those papers?" When Madge ignored his question, he made a grab for the papers. Madge pulled them closer to her.

From the landing came the booming voice of Auntie Mary.

"Children should be seen and not heard. Come on, Madge, or you'll miss the bus and we don't want that."

His Mum tried to give Andy a quick hug. He averted his face and pushed her away.

"Cheer up, I'll be back for tea," Madge said, encouragingly.

With a quick farewell to Auntie Mary, she hurried to the village centre to catch the bus.

The journey to Manchester was long and tedious. Madge failed to see any of the pretty countryside as she was pre-occupied with her own thoughts.

She alighted from the bus. She asked one or two people directions. This area was uncharted territory to her.

Crown Court in Crown Square was a large, white, imposing building. Columns interspersed the enormous windows. In the centre, at the front, was an impressive stairway. She later learned it was only used for special occasions.

Madge let out a sigh. She glanced at her watch. She slowed down. She was somewhat breathless with all her hurrying.

She entered the entrance which was to the side of the centre stairway. Security guards asked her to empty her pockets into a small container.

As she went through the control, a sharp bleep sounded. She removed the safety pin she pinned to the inside of her pocket. She sometimes used it to keep her ten pound notes safe as she pinned them to the inside of her skirt.

The lady guard ran a wand like instrument all over her. Thankfully she was clear.

Madge made her way to the District Judge's area of the County Court. In Manchester, the particular Court she needed was held in the Crown Court building.

She looked round apprehensively. She twisted her wedding ring around on her finger. Over in the corner she saw a reception desk.

She walked over and gave her name to the receptionist who took a note of her name and the case number. The receptionist asked her to go and sit down.

Madge sat down and opened the documents she was carrying. Her mind rushed from subject to subject making concentration impossible.

She heard a woman, with a rather low voice say, "hello, are you Madge Appleyard?"

Madge turned, looked up and saw a warm, plumpish lady. She had medium length brown hair which prettily framed her face. She wore a smart fashionable suit. Apart from her white blouse she was totally dressed in black – black suit, black high heeled shoes and even black stockings.

"Hello Mrs. Appleyard, I'm Sue Smith. I'm your Barrister."

"I thought Barristers wore wigs and gowns..." began Madge, somewhat surprised.

"Yes," said Sue, "but not usually in family cases. Come, let's go into this conference room and chat about the case."

Sue opened a door to a small box-like room and ushered Madge in. It was a sparsely filled room with only a table and four chairs. Sue indicated to Madge to sit down.

Sue brought out of her large black briefcase a bundle of papers around which a pink ribbon was wrapped. She opened a large blue writing book.

"I hope you don't mind but I need to make a note of what you say to help me when we go into the Court."

Sue opened up the papers in the bundle. She pointed out this was her Brief which told Sue all the facts of the case. It included any statements Madge and her husband, Mark, had made. They were apparently 'the Parties' to the case.

"I understand you and Mr. Mark Appleyard are married. You have one child called Andy," began Sue carefully.

"Yes."

"Things became bad between you and Mr. Appleyard and you separated a few weeks ago."

"Yes."

"Now you want to make sure you have what we call a Residence Order for Andy. This will enable him to live with you on a daily basis," Sue looked down at her Brief. "You don't want your husband to see Andy. You want an Order he doesn't have contact with him?"

"Yes. That's right," replied Madge with a slight catch in her voice.

"Why's that?" She asked gently as she saw Madge begin to cry.

"Well, it's a long story."

"It's alright I read about all the problems you've been having but I want to hear everything in your own words."

All the words poured out from Madge. It were as if someone had pulled the cork out of the bottle.

For many years the marriage was very happy. About two years ago, things started to change or rather Mark started to change.

He was still pleasant with other people but at home he was terrible. It was a sad tale of rows, lots of shouting, items being thrown, crockery smashed.

In more recent days, Mark hit her. Sadly, Andy was witnessing this marital disharmony.

Early on, when his parents rowed, he tried to join in. Later, when his parents started arguing, he often went off to his bedroom to get out of the way.

Madge recoiled with fear when her husband hit her. She shuddered as she recalled that dreadful car journey. She wondered where it all would lead.

She knew she could stand it no more. She decided to run away and take Andy with her.

They went and stayed in a two roomed flat. It was very comfortable and the position was ideal. However it proved to be too expensive. This was why they were now on 'holiday' with Auntie Mary. Thankfully, it was the school summer holidays.

She went to see a Solicitor to see how she stood with having Andy. She wanted to know whether there was any way she could live in her home without her husband being present.

The Solicitor advised her to start a Court action and bring what he called an Application for an Occupation Order. He told her this is where you ask the Court to make a decision that Mark has to leave the home and not return.

The Solicitor talked about asking the Court to grant another Order called a Non-Molestation Order which meant Mark would not be allowed to be violent to her or even threaten violence.

He would be ordered not to harass her. In fact, he could land up in the Criminal court if he disobeyed the Non Molestation Order.

These Orders would enable Madge to live in peace and quiet at home.

The Solicitor went on to explain there was a possibility the Court would order Mark to pay the mortgage. The Solicitor advised her to make an Application so Mark could not come and grab Andy.

He explained as they were married they were both entitled to have Andy unless the Court ordered otherwise. This meant Mark could take Andy home at any time.

The only way to stop this happening was to ensure Madge was safeguarded by a Residence Order. When Madge heard this she was very distressed.

They briefly discussed the possibility of divorce. Madge indicated she wanted to talk about that at another appointment.

For a few moments, Madge switched off as she recalled the events of the last few weeks.

She abruptly came back to reality as she heard Sue. "As I mentioned earlier you want the Court to make an Order which prevents your husband from having any contact with Andy. I have to warn you the Court is very keen children see both parents on a regular basis."

"But Mark can't. I don't ever want to see Mark again."

"I know the Court will make every effort so you and Mark don't come into contact with each other. If the Court feels Mark is a risk to Andy, contact will be supervised by volunteer workers at a contact centre," Sue gently explained.

There was a sharp knock on the conference room door. The Usher walked in.

"The Judge is waiting in Court three in the case of Madge and Mark Appleyard."

With her heart beating, Madge went into the Court. "How would all this end?" she wondered.

CHAPTER FOUR

"We're not going to get fair Justice," Pete said to Harry. "We've to escape so we can prove our innocence."

"How do you suggest we do that?" asked Harry.

"Well I've an idea," replied Pete.

"Oh, no," thought Andy, as he heard the heavy footsteps of his Auntie as she came up the stairs.

He stayed in bed after his Mother left. The less time he spent with Auntie Mary the better.

He tried to hide with his book under his bedclothes. They were rather smart bedclothes for they had pictures of various jungle animals on them. At least, Auntie Mary thought of children in that way.

However, there was no escape. His Auntie swept in like a battleship on manoeuvres into his bedroom.

"Little boys shouldn't be moping about the house," she said briskly.

"They should be out enjoying the fresh air."

Andy winced as she called him a 'little boy.' After all, he was the man of the house now Dad was not with them.

As Andy thought about his Dad he went really sad. He wondered when he could see him again. It was several weeks since he last saw him. When he tried to ask his Mum, she said they were too busy for that. He knew his Dad shouted a lot lately but he really loved him.

He particularly enjoyed it when they went swimming together. They went to a modern building with two pools. Round the outside of the pools were tables where his Mum sat. When they finished swimming, they had a snack and watched others swim. Sometimes, if the swimming pool was quiet, he was allowed in the big pool where only the grown ups went.

He remembered last time they went to the swimming pool, there was quite a bit of excitement. An elderly man was found floating on the top of the pool. Apparently, he had a heart attack and was unable to call out for help.

Fortunately, there were the swimming pool attendants sitting in a tall tower at one end of the pool. They saw him and he survived.

"Come on," said Auntie Mary forcefully, "out you go."

With a smart, deft, swift move she pulled his bedclothes off - lions, tigers and leopards all mingled on the floor. It was a good job he managed to grab his pyjama trousers in time or they would have come off too.

I guess there was one enjoyable aspect about Auntie Mary's. She made a huge breakfast full of all the things Andy liked. Andy was hardly able to move after all the egg, bacon, sausage, tomatoes, mushrooms, baked beans and fried bread he had for his breakfast.

At least, that was what Andy understood he had, but as Auntie Mary was a Vegetarian, some of what he ate was not what he thought!

After breakfast, Andy reluctantly obeyed Auntie Mary and went outside to play. He knew her better than to make a fuss and today he had no Mum to back him up.

The fact it was a lovely sunny day failed to cheer Andy. He slouched around for a few minutes. He kicked his best black shoes against some large white rockery stones in the garden. I suppose his shoes were in terminal decline as he was growing very fast. He longed to be as tall as his Dad.

What was he going to do all day? It seemed for ever until the next meal.

A light coloured frog jumped over his foot and made him start. He wondered if he could catch it. Perhaps it would be better than a prickly hedgehog for his cousin's bed.

A gleam came into his eyes as he remembered his Mum telling him hedgehogs were full of fleas, in fact, some hedgehogs have nearly a thousand fleas. She told him they get their fleas from their Mum in the nest. A slow smile crept across his face as he thought of his cousin.

His eye followed a pretty butterfly which was sitting on a dandelion. As it closed its wings, it resembled a dead leaf.

He made a mental note to tell Mr. Griffiths, his teacher, it was a small tortoiseshell.

Although many confused it with the Red Admiral because of its bright red, orange colour, Andy knew better. The dark borders on its wing with the blue crescents around the outer edge were the clue. Mr. Griffiths would be pleased, as it was becoming rare nowadays.

Seeing the tiny butterfly gave him an idea. He remembered Mr. Griffiths told them butterflies liked the smell of vanilla above all other smells. He ran back into the house.

"Auntie Mary, Auntie Mary," he called out enthusiastically. "Please may I have a vanilla ice-cream?" he asked hopefully.

"An ice cream at nine in the morning?" She said, as she bustled into the kitchen.

"Yes, Auntie, it's an experiment for school."

"Well, I've never heard the like." Although a country girl herself, Auntie Mary was quite nonplussed by this request.

"Yes, Auntie Mary. Our teacher Mr. Griffiths told us butterflies like the smell of vanilla best of all smells."

Auntie Mary toyed with the idea of giving him some of her precious vanilla essence. She decided an ice-cream would be cheaper. It should keep him out from under her feet for an hour or two.

"Here you are." She handed him a generously large ice-cream in a tub. Auntie Mary always thought in large portions.

Filled with joy his idea worked, Andy was about to dash outside with his large ice cream when Auntie Mary handed him a notebook and pen.

"Write down the results of your interesting experiment."

Once outside it was a case of a drop of ice-cream on a tall, stately, blue delphinium followed by a big lick for him, another drop of ice cream on the floribunda rose with its salmon, orange, pink, yellow blend of colours and another big lick for Andy, a drop of ice cream on a pink petunia and so on.

Having set up his experiment, he wondered what he to do as he waited for butterflies to come. He saw a large dragon fly with its beautiful multicoloured translucent wings. It looked like a helicopter as it landed on the grass.

Helicopter…. "Oh." he thought, "I wonder how Pete and Harry are doing in the Court."   He wondered if they had been able to escape. "I wish I'd brought my book out here." He murmured to himself.

He glanced across to his vanilla flavoured flowers. He saw another small tortoiseshell butterfly. It seemed to do a little dance and line itself up: its back faced the sun as if it were sunbathing. Andy made a mental note of this important piece of information. It might help him when he was on an adventure.

It was always Andy's secret dream he would be on an adventure. But nothing ever happened to him. He filed this data with other bits of knowledge he carefully preserved.

One of his titbits of information was rabbits always run upwards. If ever he were hungry, he would get his friend to clap their hands at the bottom of the hill. He would wait at the top of the hill and catch the rabbits.

Once more, he put a note in his notebook. If the experiment were successful, he might get another gigantic ice-cream in the morning. At least he could always hope.

He was very pleased his experiment was working well. He was very happy the first page of the notebook was filling up fairly rapidly.

A shiny, black beetle scurried by and made his way into the undergrowth.

A grey squirrel ran in front of Andy. Andy chased it deep into the garden. The squirrel scuttled up a tree. Andy followed it with his eyes and watched it for quite a few minutes.

As he was about to turn back, he saw something he had not seen the day before. It was a small, wooden, and broken down lean-to. Most of it was covered by overhanging branches from the neighbouring trees which made a very good camouflage.

Andy decided to go and explore. He walked over to the lean-to. He gently prised open the door and entered.

A pile of old deck chairs were stacked up in the corner. Next to them a dirty white metal garden table which saw better days and a few rusty garden tools. Over in the corner was a heap of tarpaulin.

He turned to leave when he heard a slight movement, "I bet it's another frog." He looked round to see where the frog was.

He was puzzled. Something was not right. It hit him, - what was wrong with the place. The place was devoid of spiders' webs.

The determination of his walk belied his beating heart. He pulled at the tarpaulin. He was unable to shift it. He tugged again to no avail. He bent down to look more carefully.

As his eyes adjusted to the darkness, he saw a hook and a catch in the darkest corner. He pulled them apart.

He carefully shifted the tarpaulin to one side. To his astonishment, he found a door in the floor.

He lifted the door. He saw what looked like a large rabbit hole. It was large enough for him to get down.

He was unsure what to do next. He could really do with a torch. Curiosity got the better of him.

He was about to go down the hole when he heard his Auntie Mary.

"Andy, where are you, I've been calling you for about fiveminutes. Your meal is getting cold."

CHAPTER FIVE

"Our only hope is when we're in the main Court House," said Pete, "I know the toilet area isn't very secure. We must get into the cubicles. When I cough, we can both climb out of our respective windows at the same time."

Madge entered the lightly coloured Court room with some trepidation. It was much smaller than she expected. All round the room were bookcases filled with books. On the walls were a few pictures of old Manchester.

At one end there was a large window in front of which were two tables in a T shape. Across the top of the T sat an official looking gentleman. This was District Judge Henson.

On his table were a computer, a printer and a very large computer monitor. At the side of him were some more legal books. In front of him was a bundle of papers.

He was about sixty with dyed brown, wavy hair and a rather squarish face. Most striking were his deep-set blue eyes. In fact, he was quite good looking.

He was solidly built. By his hand, he had a pair of glasses for reading.

"Come in Mrs. Appleyard." He motioned her to sit down at the end of the other table. Madge tried to ignore Mark as he sat down beside her. Sue Smith placed herself along one side of their table. Harry Jones, Mark's Barrister, sat down opposite Sue.

In time honoured way Sue began.

"If you please, Sir, I appear on behalf of the Mother in this case and My Learned Friend Mr. Jones appears for the Father."

It was a quaint tradition for Barristers to call each other 'My Learned Friend.' Quite bizarrely, if the other Lawyer were a Solicitor, they would call them 'My Friend.' This happened irrespective of the age and experience of the opposing Lawyer.

Leafing through her papers Sue pulled out a document headed Chronology.

"Sir, have you a copy of the Chronology?"

"Yes," replied DJ Henson, somewhat sharply.

"Well, Sir, you will see the parties have one child: Andy aged eight. The Mother wants residence of Andy. She wants him to live with her full time. She does not want Mr. Appleyard to have contact with Andy."

"You will have to put some powerful arguments to persuade me to prevent a Father having contact with his son," interjected DJ Henson. "The Court of Appeal has said the test is whether there is any cogent reason why a parent should not see their child."

Sue could see she was going to have a battle with the Judge.

"Yes, I appreciate that. In this case the Mother has deep concerns as to the danger the Father poses. I invite the Court to consider stopping contact or at least make certain there is adequate supervision in a Contact Centre."

She glanced down at her papers.

"As you know, Sir, there is also an application for an Injunction against Mr. Appleyard to stop him being violent towards Mrs. Appleyard, not to molest or pester her. Mrs. Appleyard seeks an Occupation Order to prevent the husband from returning to live at the matrimonial home so she can return home safely. She wants the Order extended to prevent Mr. Appleyard returning within a hundred yards of the home."

DJ Henson looked at the parties intently as if he could see into their innermost being.

Briefly, Sue outlined the facts of the case and gave a summary of all that had happened in the last two years.

"Mr. Jones what do you have to say to all of this?" The Judge asked.

Mr. Jones was a willowy, fair haired fellow with a vixen shaped face. He hid his six feet five inches well when he was seated. He was very experienced in family matters and had a very good reputation for success. However, he tended to be rather brusque with the opposition.

He opened his case for the Father.

"This is a case where the parties have been married for some twenty three years. Neither the Court nor the Social Services have been involved with the family previously. As you mentioned, the Courts encourage children to have contact with the other parent.

Further, it is a Draconian measure to evict a man from his home."

He was about to take another breath to launch into a full attack when the Judge interrupted him.

"Would your client be prepared to give an Undertaking, a promise, to the Court not to be violent or molest or pester Mrs. Appleyard without any admissions as to the allegations against him?"

Mr. Jones turned to Mark and had a quiet word with him.

"Sir, he agrees to an Undertaking not to be violent or molest or pester Mrs. Appleyard. He is not prepared to vacate the matrimonial home."

Judge Henson twisted his pen as he thought.

"Mr. and Mrs. Appleyard, tell me why Andy is not living at home with you both?

Together Madge and Mark said, "we."

"One at a time, you go first Mr. Appleyard. Do you want your wife back?"

"I don't know why she left."

Madge interrupted him, "you're unbearable."

Mark retorted, "who cared for you all these years?"

Quickly, Madge responded, "you only think of yourself nowadays."

"No, I don't."

Judge Henson interrupted them, "stop bickering."

Turning to Sue the Judge said

"Miss Smith this is a half hour Directions appointment, I am not prepared to cause a man to leave his own home on the two incidents of violence you recount in your Client's statement even if I should believe your Client in preference to Mr. Appleyard. But, if the car driving incident is true, I regard it very seriously.

However, at this stage I am neither prepared to stop contact nor require it to be supervised. I will make Directions as to what Witness statements the Parties and their witnesses can make.

I will order a report by an Officer from CAFCASS (Children and Family Court Advisory and Support Service.) They will visit the parties and interview Andy, after which they will report to the Court in fourteen weeks time. They will assist the Court by recommending where is the best place for Andy to live and as to the best level of Contact.

I now want you, Mr. Jones, and the Parties to discuss suitable days for contact which is to include Andy staying overnight on two nights each week with Mr. Appleyard."

Madge could hardly believe her ears. The Judge paid no attention to her nor did he want to hear her side of things. Panic welled up within her.

They all trooped out of the Court. Madge went back to her conference room. She presumed Mark went to another.

She saw through the window the two Barristers and their instructing solicitors in the large waiting area. They were discussing animatedly.

Sue came into the conference room.

"I'm sorry, Madge. I'm afraid we're stuck with what District Judge Henson has said. We need to sort out which days Andy can see his Father."

Madge did not know what to think or to say. She was not in the mood for compromise. All she wanted was Mark out of the house and Andy living with her.

How would she cope seeing Mark twice a week?

Sue explained all this was a temporary measure until the Court had a report from the Officer to help it.

"I don't want to see Mark. Can Mark see Andy without my having to meet him?" replied Sue, "what I need to know is whether there is a neutral ground where Andy could meet his Father."

"I suppose Mark could pick Andy up from school and drop him back there again of a morning."

After further discussion, Madge settled on Andy going to see his Father Tuesday night after school.

His Father would take him to school on Wednesday mornings. His Father could pick up Andy on Friday from School and Andy would stay overnight.

"How could Andy get home on Saturdays without me seeing Mark? Another problem is school holidays."

Madge was still worried about the arrangements. She could not think of how Andy could see his Dad without her involvement.

It was not as if Andy were a parcel and you could use a courier firm. Quite a few Judges thought some parents acted as if that were the truth.

"Isn't there any safe place where he could leave Andy and you could call later?" asked Sue.

At first, no place came to mind then Madge had inspiration.

"Andy loves swimming. If Mark took him swimming, I could pick Andy up from there."

"Yes, that sounds fine. I'll check with Mark's Barrister to see if it's alright. I'll ask the Court if we can have an early hearing date, perhaps next week, to see if we can get you back into the matrimonial home."

Sue went across to talk with Harry. Sue always found him hard work to deal with. He firmly stood his ground. He failed to grasp family cases were all about negotiation and compromise.

Thankfully, they managed to agree on the contact details. However, there was no way Mark was going to vacate the home. They had no remedy but go back before District Judge Henson.

Again Sue went first.

"Sir, you will be pleased to know we have agreed on an Interim Order regarding contact subject to your approval. However, the parties still do not agree on the occupation of the matrimonial home. I am firmly instructed by Mrs. Appleyard she cannot live in the home at the same time as Mr. Appleyard, even with an Injunction or Undertaking."

District Judge Henson considered the matter. He was pleased they agreed on interim contact.

"When does Andy go back to school?" He asked.

"In five weeks time."

The Judge glanced down at the papers.

"I will arrange an early hearing to deal with the Occupation part of the case, and any effect on family finances that decision will involve."

He picked up his telephone and had a short conversation.

"The Court listing office tells me they are able to list the case in three weeks time. I have to tell you on the facts of this case your client, Miss Smith, will have an uphill struggle to persuade me Mr. Appleyard will have to leave his home.

Perhaps, when the Court has the benefit of reading the CAFCASS Officer's report in about three and a half months time, and if, and I emphasise, if, the Court decides Andy can live with his Mother, I might have a different view."

Madge's heart dropped into her boots. How could she go home with Mark living there? Quite honestly, even a week was too long with her sister. She wondered what Andy would say when she told him he might have to change school and they may have to live at Auntie Mary's for months.

CHAPTER SIX

"Oh, I've twisted my ankle," said Harry, as his feet hit the ground. It was a much greater drop than they expected.

In spite of the pain, Harry and Pete ran like mad to the safety of the trees.

Madge's mind was in a whirl when she left Sue Smith. As she hurried through the waiting area, Mark pursued and grabbed her.

"Madge, listen to me. We need to work it out for Andy's sake."

She roughly pushed Mark's arm away.

"If you really love Andy, you would let us come home."

"That's what I want. I want you to come home. Come home with me now." He pleaded.

"No you must leave. I can't take anymore."

With tenderness, Mark replied, "I love you, Madge. It's been unbearable these last few   weeks."

He tried to put his arm on hers. She sharply pushed his arm off and moved away.

"You should have thought about that before you hit me and drove like a lunatic."

"Madge, please forgive me."

"If you meant it, you would leave home and let Andy and me return."

"You know I can't do that."

"How selfish can you get?"

Madge rushed off. She fled into the lift. She could hardly see the buttons in the lift as tears blurred her eyes. She wanted to guarantee Mark was unable to catch up with her again.

Tears streamed down her face and she bumped into people in the Court corridors. She almost stumbled as she fled through the large swing doors. The warm air hit her as she emerged into Crown Square.

As she made her way up to Deansgate, she kept thinking of the events of the last few hours. They kept going over and over in her mind. She could hardly make sense of everything.

Her heart was very heavy inside. She knew it was important Andy knew his Dad but she did not want to see Mark ever again.

Mark hit her once before but claimed it was an accident. He said he tripped and fell against her. But significantly, it happened after he said, "I've told you Madge, I expect to have my meal on the table when I come in. I work hard enough in the day. Surely, it's the least a man can expect."

I guess it was chatting to Mrs. Snoopy, as she called her next door neighbour, that made her late.

It was the last straw when, after the disastrous car ride, he pinned her against the wall. This time it was no accident. He slapped her once across the face. It was a fairly lightweight slap. What really worried her was the look in his eyes. It was a look which caused her to tremble.

Mark seemed so quick to lose his temper nowadays. It was like walking on eggshells all the time. She was not going to stay around for another round of rows. Seeing that look in his eyes, she no longer felt safe in her own home.

Now the Court was saying she must make Andy available for contact with his Dad. She could not believe the Court would say such a thing.

She kept thinking about Andy being with Mark. It was true Mark never hit Andy. Perhaps, he would be safe with him. Although there were times she was not sure. That nightmare car drive could have killed them all.

Mark was acting so strangely lately. She did not want a regular reminder of Mark himself.

Madge was deep in thought. She stepped off the kerb to cross the road. She failed to see the red sports car coming round the corner. There was a screech of brakes, a scream and deathly stillness.

The piercing sound of sirens penetrated the heavy silence as they passed Madge. The Doppler Effect was clearly heard.

The ambulance arrived. The wail of further sirens announced the appearance of the Police.

The ambulance came to a sharp halt. It backed up. The paramedics emerged and flung back the rear doors.

The control office at the Police Station received an emergency 999 call from a mobile phone.

The caller was very distressed and kept mumbling, "she's dead; I know she's dead, she just stepped out in front of me."

The Police later ascertained he was the driver of the car which hit Madge.

Police cars were sent to the scene of the accident. The first car of Police officers to arrive screeched to a halt. The officers threw themselves out of their vehicles.

The Police Officers pushed back the crowd which was gathering. They needed to enable the paramedics to get near the apparently lifeless form of a middle aged lady lying on the road fairly near the kerb.

The paramedics squatted down on the ground alongside Madge. They placed their fingers against her neck, under the chin. They faintly felt a pulse. She was barely alive.

They kept asking, "what's your name, what's your name?" They did not get any response.

One of her legs was severely injured. They bandaged the two legs together. On the ground was quite a bit of blood.

They cleared the gravel from her forehead and applied a bandage to her head. They put on a neck brace in case she had injured her spine.

It was quite clear she was very badly injured. They placed her very carefully on the stretcher and put her in the ambulance.

Once more, the sirens and flashing blue light were activated. The ambulance set off. It weaved in and out of the traffic. Cars rapidly pulled into the side of the road out of its way.

Cautiously, they negotiated the traffic signals which were on red. They arrived at the local hospital which was put on alert to expect a serious road traffic accident case.

The large automatic doors flung open as medical staff ran out to meet the ambulance.

Carefully, they took Madge out of the ambulance. They wheeled the stretcher into the accident and emergency part of the hospital.

Once inside the hospital, they took her into a small cubicle.

"One, two, three," they said in unison as they transferred Madge onto the waiting stretcher. They covered her in a red blanket.

The Doctor examined her. He authorised her removal to the operating theatre. The paramedics ran alongside the swiftly moving stretcher. They explained the background of the case. This was the end of their involvement in this matter. They rushed off to deal with another call.

Meanwhile, the Police Officers remained behind at the scene of the accident. They began by interviewing the driver of the car who hit Madge. When they saw a slim young lad of about nineteen, his hair almost shaved off, an ear ring in his left ear, the Police assumed he was at fault.

However, another man came forward from out of the crowd. He corroborated the driver's version. The lady stepped off the kerb into the road without looking.

"She obviously didn't know her Green Cross Code," thought one of the Officers.

It was unlikely the driver would be charged with any criminal offence. It was still necessary for the Officers to interview him and any witnesses.

They took careful measurements of the road. They particularly noticed where the debris and glass fell in a small pile on the road. This indicated the point of impact.

Meanwhile, at the hospital, Madge was rushed into surgery. She had an emergency operation on her legs. The big worry was she might lose one of her legs. One leg had taken the impact of the accident. The deep concern was she was still unconscious.

She was transferred from the operating theatre to intensive care.

A few days later, Madge opened her eyes. She tried to sit up. She felt as if her body had a massive weight attached which held her down.

She realised various tubes were attached to her wrists. Her legs were in plaster with a pulley holding them in the air.

Her legs throbbed dreadfully. She had a searing pain in her left arm. Her head felt as if it were on fire. She saw a young lady Police Officer sitting by her bed.

Police, tubes, legs in a pulley: what had happened? She tried to speak, nothing came. She saw the Police lady look at her. She tried to speak, to no avail.

At first, she was perplexed as to where she was. Gradually, she realised she was in a hospital bed. What had happened? How had she got here? How seriously poorly was she? As she thought about this, a Doctor came in.

"Good morning Officer," Doctor Stephen Tinsley said.

He was one of the younger Doctors. He had excelled at medical school. In fact he had one of the highest marks in the country in his year. He was well over six feet tall. He was slimly built.

"I'm afraid you're wasting your time here, it will be a long time before this lady speaks, if ever."

Madge could hardly believe what she was hearing.

"She's in a deep coma. The longer she's in the coma the worse the brain damage will be. She's already been tested on the Glasgow Coma Scale. The results do not bode well for the future."

"Brain damage," thought Madge. "I can hear everything being said, why can't I tell them this?" She wanted to cry. Tears froze in her eyes.

"We've been making enquiries. Thankfully, Mrs. Appleyard had some Court papers on her which helped us. She also had a torn up letter in her pocket which gave us more information," said PC Scotforth.

"The Father works at a chemical factory near Chorley. Apparently Mrs. Appleyard recently left him. She had gone to stay at her sister's home. We understand their young son is at that sister's home."

"What's going to happen to the boy?" asked Doctor Tinsley.

"We've informed Social Services who are going round to see him at the Auntie's." PC Scotforth replied.

"At least that will be a worry off Mrs. Appleyard's mind to know her son is being taken care of." Replied Doctor Tinsley

Madge listened with increasing horror. All she wished to do was to get back home to see Andy was alright. If she could have seen the future she would have been even more concerned to get home to Andy.

CHAPTER SEVEN

Their only hope was to get away from the Court area as fast and as quietly as they could. Their big worry was the Police would bring out their dogs.

Mark looked at his alarm clock in shock. How could he have missed the alarm going off? He threw himself out of bed. Flung on his clothes. He ran round the house like a scalded chicken. He grabbed a sandwich and ate as he checked his briefcase. He slammed the door behind him and rushed out of his home.

He could not believe it: today of all days. His car rolled over and nearly died. The best it managed was a whirr, whirr, and whirr. He knew it was an old car but it was faithful up to now.

He tinkered under the bonnet. He tried again and nothing happened. He dried all the plugs and the carburettor. It still wouldn't go. He rushed back into his home for a can of spray. It was at times like this he would have called out and

Madge would have found it instantly.

He rummaged through boxes. There it was. He ran out again to the car. He rapidly sprayed everything in sight. He tried again. A flood of relief rushed through him when the car went.

He found life much harder now Madge and Andy had left. All those little jobs Madge did for him which he took for granted. Even what he called dustbin management was a time consuming chore.

As he left for work, Madge had his briefcase ready for him with his lunch time sandwiches. A quick kiss and he would be on his way.

His heart lurched as he thought of Madge and Andy and all those kindnesses. He desperately wanted to see Madge and Andy. He had tried to phone her a number of times. He had asked to see Andy but she had refused to let him. The telephone calls were short and acerbic. Oft times, Madge would put the phone down on him.

"No, not the traffic lights," Mark accelerated and went through them on amber as they were turning to red. He drove fairly quickly out of town. He travelled along winding country roads. He glanced at his watch. Work was in sight. What a relief. He had just made it.

After parking somewhat badly, he walked across to the long, low one storey, prefabricated building. It was hurriedly built during the War. It looked very ordinary from the outside with its small, pokey windows. The only unusual feature was some small cylindrical pieces of metal sticking up through the grass.

He showed his pass a number of times. They needed a high level of security at Braders.   He arrived at the lift. He felt as if he were descending into the bowels of the earth.

Here the main work was done in underground rooms which stretched for quite a distance. It was quite a long walk from the lift to the final barrier. In some areas there were underground trolleys you could sit in which propelled along a rail. Mark knew it was quicker to walk.

Mark had to go through a number of barriers and input a code. The last requirement was for Mark to put his hand into a machine to check his palm print. He was through security.

He was pleased to have this employment as the pay was double his previous job. He found it very interesting work.

He remembered, as a little boy, he spent all his pocket money on chemical apparatus. He rushed to a local chemist as soon as he received his pocket money. The chemist had quite an array of equipment.

He did experiments in a small brick outhouse in the garden. He set up an array of apparatus on a bench.

He trawled through various books he borrowed from the library. He meticulously followed their experiments.

Whenever his Mum came in, she complained.

"This place always smells as if a stink bomb has been set off."

Quite remarkably, he never noticed!

He enjoyed reading tantalizing tales about chemists. He would read biographies about famous scientists such Madame Curie famous for her pioneering research on radio activity. Fancy a woman getting two Nobel prizes.

He was also inspired by Dr. Ignaz Semmelweis who discovered the simple remedy of washing hands stopped the spread of puerperal fever from cadavers to women having babies. As usual these pioneers were laughed at initially.

Those experiments stood Mark in good stead, now he was a research chemist. He entered his beloved laboratory. He was surrounded by large cylindrical vessels which had pointed ends. They were all connected by pipes and tubes.

The laboratory was full of temperature and pressure gauges which he used at every stage of the operation.

He started his work of the day. Precisely heated a small batch of chemicals and made a chart of his results.

He spent about two hours making meticulous, contemporaneous notes of his hard and painstaking work.

"Coffee break calls," he murmured to himself.

As he turned to leave the laboratory, there was a knock on the door. Mark opened the small window in the door.

"Mark, Mr. Pikestaff wants you in his office straightaway."

"I wonder what the old man wants now?" mumbled Mark to himself.

"How weary, I've to get back up to the ground floor."

Mark kept grumbling to himself as he made his way back the way he came earlier that morning.

Mr. Pikestaff stood by the large window of his office looking out across the rolling Lancashire countryside. He turned sharply as he heard Mark knock.

"Come in."

Mark entered the spacious office.

"Sit down," his voice was warmer than Mark was used to.

As Mark sat down, a lady brought in a tray of tea and chocolate biscuits.

"What on earth was going on?" Mark wondered.

Mr. Pikestaff handed Mark a cup of tea and pointed to the biscuits.

"I've some upsetting news to share with you, Mark. It concerns your wife."

Mark's head buzzed round.

"Unfortunately, she's been in a car accident. She's in hospital in Manchester."

Mark could hardly take it all in as Mr. Pikestaff filled Mark in with all the details. All he could think of was how he could get to see Madge.

"Clearly, you can take time off to go and see your wife."

"Thank you, Sir. May I go now?"

Mr. Pikestaff paused and ran his teeth over his lower lip. He inwardly winced as he wondered how Mark would take what he had to say.

"Well that's the other problem."

By now, Mark was slouched in his seat with worry. At this, he shot bolt upright.

"Andy is alright isn't he?"

"Yes. He's alright. No, the problem is ours. Here at the Plant."

"Now what was coming?" Mark wondered. "Was he about to give him the sack as well?"

"The problem is we need you to go on your overseas conference trips." Mark thought for a minute. His mind darting between visions of Madge in hospital, who could he get to help him look after Andy and these wretched conferences.

Mark wondered how Mr. Pikestaff dare discuss these matters at such a time. He knew he was a hard-nosed business man who had little regard for feelings but he thought at a time like this he might have been more human.

"Couldn't Roger go? He's been involved in much of my experiments."

Mark could see by Mr. Pikestaff's face he was wasting his time. He was a businessman through and through. In fact, Mark was surprised he had shown the compassion he had.

Mark was reluctant to lose his job. But he needed to see Madge as often as he could and ensure Andy was cared for. Mark decided on another tack.

"If I go on these conference trips could I have extra time off to see my wife?"

Mr. Pikestaff thought about it for a minute or two.

"Yes."

Mark decided to seize the moment.

"Could I have a ten percent uplift on my salary for the next four months to help with all the extra costs I'm going to face?"

Mr. Pikestaff was unhappy about this idea.

"I'm prepared to pay you double during the time you are on the trips."

Mark's heart sank to his boots. How was he going to manage? All the extra travelling and Andy's day to day care.

He had recently ordered and splashed out on a new car. If he had known this was all coming he would have waited. Although, the morning's problems with his present car proved he had done the right thing.

Mark knew it was no use arguing with Mr. Pikestaff so reluctantly agreed.

With a very heavy heart, Mark left Mr. Pikestaff's office and rushed back to the laboratory for his belongings.

He ran across to the car park and set off to see Madge.

CHAPTER EIGHT

Pete looked worried when he came off the telephone.

"The Police are at Sarah's. She's worried they'll follow her if she tries to meet us with a car. How are we going to get from this wilderness?"

A harsh, shrill ring of the telephone penetrated through Auntie Mary's house. She had a very old fashioned white telephone with a large dial on the front.

Auntie Mary bustled in from the garden where she was busy doing some sequential planting of lettuce and radish. This she did every fortnight which gave them fresh vegetables throughout all the summer months.

She remembered the time Andy visited her when he was very much smaller. Andy stayed for a week. Every day he pulled up some of the radishes to see how they were growing.

As you can imagine that particular crop of radish was exceptionally slim!

"Who could be ringing me at this time?"

She was frustrated. She had spent a couple of hours on cleaning the house during the morning. Now her hands were covered with soil.

Putting large, smudgy soil marks on her bright white telephone receiver, she said, with obvious annoyance in her voice, "yes, who is it?"

"Is that Mrs. Mary Macton?" The voice asked.

"Yes," said Auntie Mary brusquely.

"This is Central Manchester Police Station. We're ringing about a Mrs. Madge Appleyard. We understand she's your sister."

"Madge, what's the matter, she isn't hurt is she?"

"I'm sending a local officer to see you straightaway. He'll be with you in a few minutes. It's better if he explains everything to you."

Auntie Mary was deeply upset by the call. She had only time to wash her muddy hands when there was a knock at the back door.

PC Jim Johnson was the local Brockton Police Officer. He was an older officer, medium height, greyish hair and solidly built. His Police uniform was tight across his fat tummy.

He lived quite near Auntie Mary. They went to the village school together. In fact, they were in the same class. He was one of the few people who called her by her first name.

"Hello, Jim, come in." P. C. Johnson followed her into the living room.

"Mary, sit down. I'm sorry; I'm the bearer of bad news."

"Madge's not dead is she?" interrupted Auntie Mary.

"No, but she's very seriously injured."

He recounted information about the road traffic accident and Madge's hospitalisation. He tried his best but he could not soften the blow.

He had never seen Auntie Mary cry before. She sat there silently. Her head bowed. Large tears trickled down her face.

Although she was not very demonstrative, she loved her sister Madge very much and would do anything for her. It distressed her deeply, she was injured.

She lifted up her head. She wiped her eyes which now showed a defiant look in them.

"We'll manage; we'll manage, even if I've to bring Andy up myself. I'll make sure that crackpot of a Father doesn't get his hands on him."

After PC Johnson left Auntie Mary went to the back door and called.

"Andy, Andy, come in."

Andy had learned to be obedient when Auntie Mary called. He was in the house like a shot.

"Here's a piece of my Victoria sponge cake."

Andy was astonished to be given a piece of cake at that time of the day but he was not complaining.

Before Auntie Mary could explain to Andy what had happened there was a loud knock at the front door.

No-one ever knocked at her front door. Everyone came round to the back door. Many of her visitors just walked in.

She went through to the front door. She moved some of the objects which had piled up in front of the door. As she opened the door a few earwigs dropped down. A spider scurried away.

Two visitors were standing on her doorstep: a Police officer and a smartly dressed lady in a brownish green tweed suit.

The older lady spoke, "I'm Mrs. Marvin from Social Services. This is Police Woman Williams. We've come to collect Andy and take him into care."

Without giving Auntie Mary time to say anything, Mrs. Marvin strode into the house followed closely by PW Williams.

Mrs. Marvin was a well-built older lady in her early fifties. She had been with the Social Services for about twenty years.

Outwardly, she appeared gruff and overbearing perhaps even arrogant. Two nervous breakdowns were an indication of her very sensitive nature.

Only on Saturday, she investigated a case where there was an allegation of child abuse. She believed the Father had shaken the baby. The baby suffered bleeding in her eyes and some damage to the brain. She was now cared for in hospital. Thankfully, the baby would survive. Mrs. Marvin confronted the Father who denied he had done anything. He said the baby fell off the couch. This caused the injury.

It was so very difficult to get to the truth of these cases.

Everyone involved tried to protect themselves from prosecution. Often it was ignorance on the part of the parents who did not realise the severe damage they caused by shaking a baby.

When she went home and told her children they looked baffled.

"Why does shaking hurt the baby? Yet doesn't harm a woodpecker that keeps moving his head back and forward as his beak pecks at the tree?" They asked.

She confessed she did not know the answer. She resolved to ask the specialist next time she saw him.

She had a very varied job. Today, she had to take Andy into care. His Mum was seriously injured and his Dad was going abroad.

"Well, where's Andy?" She demanded.

At that moment, Andy emerged from the kitchen with a large piece of Auntie Mary's cake in his sticky hand.

"So this is Andy," PW Williams began. She was a fledgling in the force. She usually enjoyed her work but found it hard to impart bad news.

"Andy, your Mummy isn't very well. She's had an accident."

"An accident!" exclaimed Andy. His face went white beneath his sunburn.

"Where's my Mummy, I want my Mummy." He ran toward the door as if he expected her to be standing there.

"I'm sorry your Mummy's in hospital. She's very poorly. A car came round the corner and knocked her down."

At that, Andy began to cry.

As he sobbed, Auntie Mary put her arm round him. Surprisingly, he cuddled his face into her apron.

"We've come to take Andy into care," said Mrs. Marvin. "He'll go to a temporary foster home tonight."

"But why can't he stay here? This is a big house and I'm at home all day."

"Oh," said Mrs. Marvin giving a sideways glance at PW Williams. "We understood from the Father you wouldn't want Andy to stay if your sister weren't here."

"That's nonsense," snapped Auntie Mary. "Blood is thicker than water. Of course he can stay here."

Andy fled into his own world. He sobbed quietly.

"Would you like to stay with your Auntie?" asked Mrs. Marvin.

"With Auntie Mary?" a look of horror crossed Andy's face.

"Stay with Auntie Mary – alone?" he gasped. "No, I want my Mummy, I want my Daddy."

"No," Mrs. Marvin gently replied, "your Mummy is not well enough to look after you."

"I want to stay with my Daddy."

"Your Daddy is flying off to Austria to give work lectures." The other disturbing matters being investigated by the Court were not for Andy to know.

"It's either with me or strangers," added Auntie Mary.

Andy went very quiet. His brain was racing like mad. Go to strangers in a foster home? Stay with the Dragon...Auntie Mary? He would be able to see his Mum at the hospital. At least he knew the worst at Auntie Mary's.

"I'll stay with Auntie Mary," he said firmly.

"That's settled," said Mrs. Marvin. She gave her work card to Auntie Mary.

"If you have any problems or you need my help do not hesitate to call me at the office."

As they walked away down the path, Andy wondered what he had done.

CHAPTER NINE

Pete and Harry could hear the loud roar of the Police cars. They managed to hide behind the trees. They saw seven cars with flashing lights and sirens speed by.

Auntie Mary bustled round the house with her mind in a whirl. Not much fazed her.

She was called up to be a soldier during the Second World War. Whilst she was at Camp she was given the opportunity to join the Indian Army. Not long after she sailed with a troop ship to India. The ship was packed with two thousand soldiers.

Auntie Mary wrote home to tell how a commotion broke out on board the ship the first day. It was discovered Dr Major Creak had been placed in the same cabin as another Major. The ship's captain was brought in to resolve the matter. They presumed Dr Major Creak was a man. They put Dr Major Creak with another man. In fact, she was a lady Doctor - Dr. Mildred Creak who later became a famous

Psychiatrist at Great Ormond Street children's Hospital in London, England.

The family was amused to read when Auntie Mary wrote home to say she was promoted from Private to a Trooper. The joke being it was the same level of rank.

She was stationed at various camps in India. Although there was a war to be won there, not much was happening in her part of India.

A lot of time was spent in learning Urdu: an important Indian language. She was also able to visit local bazaars, which she found very colourful, and even sit out and enjoy the sunshine. Many photographs were sent home.

Whilst she was in Bombay, she met Major Dennis Macton, a tall, good-looking officer with beautiful dark curly hair and rich brown eyes. He had the most infectious of laughs. She was bowled over the first time she met him. Soon it was clear her feelings were reciprocated.

A whirlwind romance ensued. They were married soon after.

She was sent back to England to Civvy Street. Farewell at the railway station was tearful and poignant. This was the last she ever saw him. Soon afterwards, he was posted to Burma. There came that fateful telegram which bluntly announced Major Dennis Macton was killed in action.

At least, she had the certain knowledge he was killed, when so many others received notice their relative was missing, presumed dead. These were the ones who waited with lingering hope their loved one would turn up again.

She also knew she would always have something of her husband as she was having his baby. This joy turned to deep sadness when the baby died a few minutes after he was born. He was a boy. He would have been Dennis Macton junior.

Auntie Mary never got over this double tragedy. But in some ways it had made her more resilient to later problems.

Over the years she had looked at Andy with deep, motherly love in her heart and thought of her little boy. How she would have loved to have brought Andy up. "If only." She had soon learned in life it was useless to ask this question.

She looked fondly across at Andy as he sat in the big armchair reading his thriller. For a moment, softness filled her heart. Quickly, she put back her tough exterior for he belonged to Madge and Mark.

"Come on Andy," she loudly exclaimed, "it's time you were out in the garden enjoying this lovely sunny day."

Somewhat reluctantly, Andy put his book in his jacket pocket and went out of doors.

He did not feel a bit like playing. He gave the vanilla soaked flowers a cursory glance. He had no heart to make any more notes. Even thoughts of the tunnel no longer attracted him.

All he wanted to do was go and visit his Mum in the hospital. How could she leave him like this? No Dad and now, no Mum. He felt like an orphan.

He walked up and down the grassed-over pathway for a few minutes. He idly kicked stones as he walked. His mind was full of his Mum.

On the patio he found a white plastic chair. He sat down and took his paperback out of his pocket. He started to read some more about Pete and Harry but he was unable to concentrate. The words seemed to merge into each other.

"Don't look so gloomy, it may never happen." Andy looked up to see where the voice came from. He could see nothing.

"Over here." The voice tantalising called again.

This time the voice seemed to come from the opposite direction.

Andy jumped up from his chair. He looked round but could not see anything.

For a third time, the voice called out "over here." This time, it came from the first direction.

Andy spun round. He walked towards the trees. He peered into the bushes.

At first, no-one was visible because he was looking from where it was sunny to where it was dark. Little by little, he could make out the form of a boy of about the same age as himself. As he walked towards the voice he heard another voice.

"Over here." This came from deeper into the bushes.

This was too much for Andy. He felt too sad to be playing games.

He flopped back into the garden chair. Tears filled his warm, soft, brown eyes. They trickled down his face.

"Hey, we didn't mean to upset you, we were only playing a game with you."

Andy was knocked for six to see identical twins emerge from the bushes.

They were about the same age as Andy but slightly shorter. They had a shock of red hair and lots of freckles.

They were dressed identically in short shorts and wore an open-necked jumper. The only difference between the twins was one was dressed in red and the other was dressed in blue.

"I'm Sammy," said the one in red, "this is my brother Danny."

"I'm the older by half an hour that makes me the boss." He proudly proclaimed. "I'm the boss of our gang."

"Gang?" enquired Andy.

"Yes, there're three of us."

"But I can only see two of you. Are you triplets?" asked Andy somewhat mystified.

"Don't be silly," said Sammy good-humouredly. "No, the third member of the gang is Maisie. She's only a girl but she's a good fighter."

Andy looked round but he could not see anyone. Slowly, he saw the bushes part and Maisie emerged. Andy recognised her as his fierce combatant of the previous day when they had sprawled on the floor.

"Not you," said Andy and Maisie in unison.

The twins looked at each other in surprise.

"You know each other?" Sammy asked with astonishment in his voice.

"Not really." Replied Andy slowly. He was about to tell them about the skirmish they had the previous day but changed his mind.

"We've met around," he answered carefully.

"Do you live at "The Myrtles?" enquired Danny.

"No," replied Andy, "I'm only staying there for a short time with my Auntie Mary."

For a moment he hesitated whether to tell his new found friends about his Auntie and his Mum. Looking fully at Maisie he said somewhat hesitantly.

"I'll tell you a secret if you'll tell me one."

"Ok." they answered.

Andy recounted briefly why he and his Mum had come to stay with the Dragon. This was his private name for his Auntie Mary.

He told them how his Mum had a terrible accident.

He explained his Dad was going abroad and was unable to look after him.

"You poor thing," Sammy said.

"Anyway, do brighten up. You've us now; we'll become the "four musketeers." added Danny.

"What secret do you want us to tell you?" they asked.

"Well, Maisie," Andy said, "I really know the answer but I want you to tell me. How did you escape the other day?"

"It was simple really," she said light-heartedly. "I climbed a tree. It was funny watching you look for me. I nearly fell off the branch laughing."

Andy paled and looked very perplexed.

Maise looked at his face. Now it was her turn to look bemused. "I thought you said you knew how I'd escaped."

Andy took a deep breath.

He trusted them so far. He really had to trust them completely.

Bit by bit Andy explained everything to his new found friends.

Andy told how he searched to find out how Maisie escaped. He told how he found what he called the 'rabbit hole.'

"Wow," they said, "hurry, let's go and look."

CHAPTER TEN

"I'm desperate for some food," said Harry, "we haven't eaten for more than twenty four hours. I know a transport café about a mile from here. If we weave through the trees, we might be able to get there without being seen."

There was a loud knocking at Auntie Mary's back door. Auntie Mary took off her apron, straightened her hair. She went to see who knew to come to the back door yet knocked so loudly.

Mark Appleyard was about six feet tall. He was slender and stooped slightly. He had thick dark hair, which was greying at the sides. He was still a very handsome man. He was slightly sensitive about his age as he had reached forty.

Perhaps, because he knew Auntie Mary well, he was considerably nervous at the prospect of seeing her under the present situation. She had a sharp tongue when she wanted. In fact, he dreaded seeing her.

It was important to keep on the right side of Auntie Mary as he needed her help. He wanted to take Andy for days out.

"Hello Mary," he said, "may I come in?"

"Why didn't you telephone?" she asked pointedly.

"I did but you were engaged."

"Oh yes, one of my neighbours was on the phone a very long time."

She did not add, she left the phone off the hook after that. The time her neighbour had taken set her back at least an hour and she wanted to get on with her work.

"You better come in," she said coldly.

Mark went into the living room. He stood there uncomfortably not daring to sit down. Auntie Mary stood near the door with her arms folded. She glared at him.

"You're not very welcome here, Mark, after what you did to my sister."

Madge tried to be as civil as she could. At that moment she hated Mark for all he had done to her sister. Court was all his fault. Madge having to go to Court was all his fault. The accident was all his fault.

"Well, what have you come for?" she asked sharply.

"I've come to take Andy home."

"And who said you could?"

"Actually, the Court said Andy could stay with me twice a week."

"Well, I don't care what any Court says. You can only take him out for the day. I want him back for tea."

Auntie Mary put her head through the open back door and called Andy. She caught him just before he and his friends set off into the shrubs to look at the 'rabbit hole.'

"You're Dad's here." An icy sharpness in her tone was not lost on Mark.

Andy was thrilled to know he would be visiting his Mum. He was also excited at seeing his Dad. He hurriedly said goodbye to the Gang and ran into the house.

"Hi Andy," said Mark. "How would you like to go for a spin in my new car?"

"New car, Dad, wicked!" answered Andy. Now he would see his Mum. He could hardly wait for his Dad to open the back door. He ran in front of his Dad round the side of the house.

The weeks he had not seen his Dad melted away.

In the driveway was Mark's white Mercedes. It had been on order for some months as it was a prototype model. He had just taken delivery. He was very much relieved after the recent troubles he had with his old car. He looked forward to showing it off to Andy.

Andy's eyes opened wide when he saw it. "Wow, Dad, it's a sport's convertible."

They jumped into the car. Mark brought Andy a multicoloured hat and a pair of goggles. Andy put them on. Mark pressed a switch and lowered the roof. Soon they were zipping through the countryside with the wind blowing through their hair. Andy wished his friends could see him now.

Bubbling with excitement Andy asked. "We're going to see Mum, aren't we?"

"Sorry, son, the hospital said no visitors just yet."

He did not think it the moment to tell Andy the full facts and how awful it would be to see Madge with all the tubes and machines attached to her.

"But, Dad if they knew how much I want to see her, they might let me in."

"No, I'm sorry, son,"

"Well, can we go and look at her through the window?"

"No, I'm sorry"

"Why? They can't stop us doing that."

Mark hesitated. "She's on the third floor."

"No, she isn't, no she isn't, you're just saying that. I want to see her now."

"Andy, that's enough." Mark made as if he were going to hit Andy and thought better of it. "That's enough. Now what would you like to do?"

"See Mum."

Mark was desperately trying to keep his temper. "We're not going to see Mum and that's that."

They drove on for a while in silence.

Mark was perplexed what to do. He gave a quick glance at Andy. He could see the tears trickling down his face. He pulled over to the side of the road and gently put his arm round Andy's shoulder.

"I understand but sometimes in life we can't do what we want, when we want."

Andy refused to look at his Dad. He sullenly looked at the floor.

"You've a choice Andy. We can either make the best of this day out together or I can take you back to Auntie Mary's. What's it to be?"

"I love my Mum and I want to see her."

"I know. But I can't make it happen. At the moment You've only got me. I want to be with you and this is the day I can take you out. Don't let's spoil it."

Andy gave his Dad a weak smile,

"OK."

Mark set off again and travelled down some narrow country lanes. Sheep were grazing in the fields. Occasionally, a herd of cattle was to be seen.

They passed a camp where there were many one storey pre-fabricated buildings. This is where the air force was stationed during the Second World War. They went by a number of tall aerials under which were...but that must remain a secret even for this story.

They passed the old Sanatorium where many people with tuberculosis were treated. Even in winter the patients were tucked up in bed on the open verandahs.

They arrived in the pretty village of Elswick. They turned round an acute bend. They pulled up sharply to negotiate the sleeping policemen at the entrance into the car park at Bond's ice cream parlour and restaurant.

Soon Andy was settled on a tall bar seat. The ice cream bar was a delicate shade of blue. Dotted round were a number of tables and chairs.

The attendant brought him a huge Knickerbocker Glory. It was a myriad of colour with all sorts of ice-creams and fruit cocktail topped with lashings of cream. Sprinkled on the top was loads of chocolate. This was Andy's absolutely favourite dish.

He leisurely plodded his way through the sweet. He enjoyed every mouthful. At the bottom of the glass was a bright red cherry which he managed to hook out with his long spoon.

Leaving the ice-cream parlour, they drove down a very narrow lane. Unusually for that part of the country, it had thatched roof cottages. Mark parked his car in the narrow lane.

They put on their Wellingtons and walked through the fields until they reached the embankment of the river Wyre.

Andy loved going walks with his Dad. As they went along his Dad paused and pointed out particular flowers. He would give their name or he would say "shssh." They would come to an abrupt halt and listen. Andy would hear a field lark or the rarer sound of the speckled song thrush who sang its song twice over.

Andy was proud to know a lot of the names of the flowers and birds.

He knew how to tell the difference between the three main types of sparrows. He mentally listed them. There were house sparrows, hedge sparrows and field sparrows.

The hedge sparrow was not a true sparrow. Its other name was Dunnock. It had a pointed beak. The other two had a short, thick wedge-shaped beak.

A friend of his father's told him it made a difference in English law to be able to identify the correct sparrow. You could never harm the hedge sparrow as it was a protected bird.

He knew the sparrows with the black bib were male and the ones without the black bib were female.

He was good on flowers as well. He knew the red campion was for snake bites. He often rubbed a dock leaf on his legs when he was stung by a nettle. His Dad told him not to complain about nettles as it meant the soil was very rich.

He gave a wry smile to himself as he thought of the times Auntie Mary dished up nettles with his lunch telling him, "eat up my boy, they're full of iron."

Today, his Dad told him about comfrey. He knew the information would be useful when he returned to school.

He had seen the pink flowered plant with large leaves in Auntie Mary's garden. He would get her to boil him some in a pan. When he sustained a bruise playing football he would bandage it onto his leg.

After leaving the car, they scrambled up onto the embankment and set off towards Shard Bridge near Hambleton.

The tide was out. In the distance were a number of small boats and yachts firmly anchored and settled on the mud flats. Others moored to the bank further down the river.

As they meandered alongside the river, Andy thought about what had happened the last few weeks. It was almost too much to take in: leaving home, not seeing Dad, living in a flat, followed by going to Auntie Mary's, finally his Mum injured and in hospital.

Andy loved his Dad. He was very upset as weeks flew by and his Dad did not appear. He could not understand why he could not see his Dad as usual.

Andy walked alongside his Dad in silence. He was deep in thought.

At last he blurted out, "Dad, when can I go home?"

"I thought you'd agreed to enjoy our day out. Why do you want to rush back to Auntie Mary's?"

"No, not Auntie Mary's, that's not home. Home is where you and Mum and I are together: where the pull is."

"What do you mean, 'where the pull is'?" asked Mark with a quizzical look on his face.

"When you're away you want to get back home. Home seems to pull you back. It's not really home when you're not there."

"I see. You mean like gravity? It pulls you?"

"Yes, that is what I'm saying: where the pull is."

Mark was nonplussed how to answer. He knew it could be months before Madge was better.

"I know it's hard you can't see Mum and you can't come home. I tell you what. I'm going to Nice in France for a couple of days on Thursday. I only have to be at the lecture hall for one hour. You could look around near the hall whilst you're waiting for me. I'll see what Auntie Mary says about you coming with me."

"But I want to…." began Andy.

"Don't let's start all that again. It's either Nice or stay with Auntie Mary's. It's up to you."

He was unsure how Auntie Mary would respond to his request. He could not afford to fall out with Auntie Mary at the moment. It certainly irked him to ask her permission to take his own son.

Mark thought for a moment. "Let's keep it as our secret from Auntie Mary for the moment. I'll let her get over my taking you out today. We can ask her in a couple of days."

Andy brightened up at the thought of going in an aeroplane to a foreign country. What would they say when he got back to school?

Soon the day was over. They returned to Auntie Mary's home.

Mark left Auntie Mary's promptly. He did not want her to launch into battle again.

Andy followed his Dad to the car. He watched till his Dad went out of view.

Andy was sorry to see his Dad leave. His sadness was tempered by his desire to tell 'the Gang' about his visit to France. His Dad only said not to tell Auntie Mary so he knew it was alright to tell his new friends.

In his excitement he had forgotten about the 'rabbit hole.' Suddenly, it all came flooding back. Perhaps they could all go and look now.

He wanted to do a reckie (reconnoitre) as he had another plan in his mind. He reckoned without Auntie Mary.

"Andy, Andy your tea is going cold."

After his Knickerbockers Glory he had no appetite for his tea. He managed to stuff something down with great difficulty.

After tea, he decided to go and look for his friends. It hit him. How did he find them?

CHAPTER ELEVEN

After they had eaten Harry and Pete managed to hitch a lift in an open covered wagon.

It was a lovely sunny day. The sunshine streamed through the hospital window. Madge was in the bed close to the large windows. She stirred slightly.

It was a two bed ward where seriously ill patients were placed. It was attractively decorated in a cream and pale green. A Van Gogh painting, with beautiful orange sunflowers on it, hung on the wall opposite the window. At the end of Madge's bed were a number of clips holding A4 documents. These were charts and daily records of Madge's medical progress.

In the corner was a small, white wash basin. By each bed were two upright chairs. At the side of each bed was a small cabinet on wheels. This was for the patient's personal belongings. The other bed in the room was empty as the patient was discharged earlier in the week.

Sitting in a red comfortable arm chair in the ward was a nurse. On hearing Madge stir she looked anxiously on. As there was no further movement she continued with her reading.

Nurse Phillips was in her early twenties. Her long blond hair shone in the morning sunshine. It was carefully tied back. She was very pretty. Some thought she looked a bit like Marilyn Monroe, the famous film star.

She was on the lower rung of the nurses' hierarchy. She hoped over time to make her way to the top. She dreamed of being a Doctor but financial constraints at home and a young brother with muscular dystrophy meant she had to start working as soon as she could.

She loved her work at the hospital. She was always saddened when a patient was in a coma. In these types of cases there seemed so little the medical staff could do.

Madge opened her eyes. She wondered for a moment where she was. It all came rushing back – the Court, crossing the road. What happened after that? Her mind was a blank.

Her eyes focussed on her room. She saw the nurse. She must be in hospital: why? She saw the pulley attached to her legs. She wondered how badly she was hurt. She felt various tubes attached to her arm. These tubes were attached to a tall machine by her bed.

Where was Andy? Who was looking after him? Madge became agitated as she worried what had happened to him. Who was looking after him? Painfully, the thought came to her it might be Mark.

The thought of Mark caused her mind to centre on the problems of recent days.

Gradually, she remembered: the plan she formulated as she left the Court.

She was determined to prevent Mark from seeing Andy until the CAFCASS report came through. If her devious plans went well, Andy would say he did not want to see his Father. She would probably win when the final hearing at Court decided whether Andy could have contact with his Father.

The first part of her plan was quite simple. She would appear to be as helpful as possible. Every time Andy was supposed to have contact with his Dad, she would make sure it did not happen. She would say Andy was ill or had to go to a party or they had made other arrangements for the day. She would make sure she let everyone know at the last minute so there was no time to do anything about it.

The second part of her plan was very much more difficult, particularly in the short time available to her. She only had until the time the Officer came to interview Andy to turn Andy against his Dad so he no longer wanted to see him.

She had done a bit of psychology at night school. She knew she must get Andy to champion her. She would keep telling him he was 'the man of the house' now. She would make sure she got very distressed when Mark's name was mentioned. She would tell him of any bad things which had happened during the marriage. She would make sure she magnified them. Every week, she would tell Andy his Dad had not bothered to come.

She inwardly smiled at the powerfulness of her idea. She would make sure she picked up the phone first. It was important she grabbed the post before Andy. The post was easy in term-time as it arrived after Andy had gone to school. It was going to be more difficult in the holiday time.

She needed Auntie Mary to help her whilst they were staying there. Madge hoped against hope their stay at Auntie Mary's would be short.

Yes, she would turn Andy against his Dad and nobody would even know how scheming she was.

She gave no thought how her plan would affect Andy. The long term damage it would cause. Perhaps affect his relationship-making with others. What would he think when he was older when he realised what she had done? He may even turn against her. No, none of these considerations were in Madge's mind.

For the moment, it was vital she left the hospital. Madge looked fixedly at the nurse. She tried to form words but nothing came. Suddenly, it was if a bomb went off, as the word, "Andy," exploded from her lips.

The nurse shot up her head, her book fell noisily to the floor. She looked at Madge's still form in bed. She jumped up, ran to the door, looked up and down the corridor and spotted Doctor Tinsley.

"Doctor, Doctor," Nurse Phillips called, "come quickly. Madge Appleyard has spoken."

Whirling round to face the young breathless nurse, he looked at her with astonishment. He walked purposefully down the corridor. He swept past Nurse Phillips with hardly a glance and looked carefully at Madge.

The pink flush on Nurse Phillips face should have told him more. Whenever Anne Phillips saw Doctor Tinsley she suffered an inward mixture of love and awe.

He was the pin-up of every nurse. Six foot two, short cropped blond hair, with a slight wave at the front. He had a lithe sportsman like figure. As one of his hobbies was athletic training, this was no wonder.

He was equally charming whether he was dealing with patients or the medical staff. Everyone wanted to be on the ward when Dr Tinsley was about. It was even known for people to change shifts so they could work with him.

Dr Tinsley was more concerned with his patients than lovelorn nurses. Although, it has to be said, he enjoyed the warm attention he always received.

He looked down at Madge's still figure. He was about to turn away when he thought better of it. He took out a small silver coloured torch from his breast pocket. As he looked into her eyes, Madge stirred again. She sat bolt upright, her eyes staring, and exclaimed.

"Andy, Andy where are you?" Exhausted, she flopped back against the bright white pillows.

Doctor Tinsley took hold of her hand.

"It's alright, Andy is alright."

Slowly, Madge turned her head. Doctor Tinsley saw there was a spark of recognition in her eyes.

At long last the coma was over. Now was the long haul to recovery. She was deeply unconscious for nearly a week. He was worried as to the extent of brain damage.

.

CHAPTER TWELVE

"The cops have been busy in our area,"
said the old man driving the wagon. He looked
carefully at Harry and Pete as he continued.
"They've a road block a mile up the road."

"Auntie Mary, may I look at your books?" Andy had a plan, a very secret plan.

"Of course, but I thought you're reading about Pete and Harry."

She was secretly pleased Andy was a good reader. She loved to encourage children to read books. She had quite a few children's books in her home.

"Yes, but I want another book lined up for when I've finished."

He wandered leisurely into her front room. He did not want to give anything away by rushing. Once inside, he rapidly chose a book he thought he would enjoy.

Now came the real task. Laboriously, he searched through the books. There was one type of book he was looking for. After much searching, he found it.

Somewhat crinkled and well folded. It was a map of the area. He hid the map underneath the rather large book he had chosen and shot up to his bedroom.

Very carefully, he spread out the map on his chest of drawers. He had the forethought to pick up Auntie Mary's magnifying glass so he could see even the smallest detail.

At first, he was confused. Eventually, he realised it showed the main roads. There were green lines which said they referred to underground works. He worked out red blobs were hospitals. He looked at the map intently until he found the hospital where his Mother was.

Next, he searched for Auntie Mary's village. He scrutinised the map until he found Auntie Mary's garden. He found the start of the tunnel in Auntie Mary's lean-to. He traced the tunnel line until he found the end.

He realised it cut a sizeable chunk off his journey if he used the tunnel. He folded up his map.

The next part of his plan was more difficult to accomplish. He needed to go into Auntie Mary's kitchen without her knowing. He waited until she went into the garden to collect vegetables.

He hurried into the kitchen. He gathered some bread, a tomato and put a blob of ketchup on the bread. He grabbed a slice of her cake and a bottle of fruit juice.

He was clever enough to take a bottle from behind the others so Auntie Mary would not notice the missing bottle.

As he saw her returning, he hastily grabbed an apple and shot upstairs to his bedroom. He made up his sandwiches and stuffed all the food into his rucksack.

He hardly slept that night as he thought about what he was going to do. He kept thinking about his Mum. He wanted to give her a big hug and cuddle up to her. Just feel her close to him. He was frightened of over-sleeping. Eventually he fell asleep.

The next morning, Andy woke with a start. He jumped out of bed and dressed rapidly. He pulled his rucksack onto his back and crept out of the house.

The blackbird was starting the dawn chorus with his beautiful, mellow song.

He looked round furtively as he crossed Auntie Mary's garden. He reached the lean-to. He darted inside.

He opened his rucksack to have one last quick check. Yes, there was the old map he found at Auntie Mary's. On top of the map was the food.

He remembered to include his novel, in case he had to wait before he saw his Mum. His pyjamas were in there, so he could stay overnight. At the side of the sandwiches was his torch.

He bent over and removed the tarpaulin. He lifted up the door. He shone his torch onto the ledge. He tried to descend. It was too cumbersome with the rucksack on his back. It was getting wedged.

He struggled out again. He took his rucksack off. He put it at the edge of the hole. He grabbed his torch which he held in one hand. He grabbed the rucksack with the other. He reached the first ledge. He was about to descend to the next ledge when the torch light flickered and went out.

Frustrated, he scrambled out of the hole. He put his rucksack on. He crept out through Auntie Mary's garden.

With some difficulty, he clambered over the gate. He knew he dare not open it, as it squeaked. He set off walking down the road.

After a while, he paused and shifted the weight of the rucksack. He gave his legs a quick rub and plodded on.

After about two hours, he sat down by the road side. He was feeling pretty exhausted.

He opened the packet of food he prepared. He ate a tomato sandwich. He was glad he remembered to put some ketchup on it. He followed this with a large piece of Auntie Mary's cake and a swig of apple juice. He felt a bit brighter after eating.

He picked up his rucksack and threw it on his back and continued his journey.

The rain came down in torrents. Andy pulled his hood over his head. He tried to jog down the road. He felt so weary. He wondered how much further he had to go.

All he could think about was his Mum lying injured in hospital.

The words pumped through his brain. "I have to get there. I have to get there."

The adrenalin flowing through him helped to ease his tiredness. His feet hurt.

Suddenly, there was a screech of brakes as a car pulled alongside him.

"Get in, get in at once," his Dad screamed at him.

Andy ran as fast as he could down the road. His rucksack bobbled on his back.

Mark followed him in the car. He swerved into the side of the road just ahead of Andy.

Andy looked wildly round. On his left was a five bar gate into a field where cows were grazing. Andy scrambled over it. He dashed across the field.

Mark shot out of his car and gave chase. He rugby- tackled Andy and brought him down to the ground. They wrestled in the mud and cow dung.

Mark pushed Andy's arm up his back and frogmarched him back to the car. He roughly pushed him in the car and put his seat belt on him.

"Don't you ever dare do that again, what do you think you were doing? Auntie Mary and I were sick with fear."

"I want to see Mum."

"I've told you the hospital said you can't see her. They won't even let me see her. You're coming with me to France."

"I don't want to go to France. I won't go to France. "

"I don't care what you want; you're coming to France with me on Thursday."

Andy looked at his Dad very sullenly.

Mark continued, "I'm already running late for an appointment."

"Is it about Mum?"

"Just be quiet. You've caused enough trouble for one day. If you try to run away again, Welfare will lock you up."

They journeyed on in silence. They reached Auntie Mary's home.

Mark held Andy firmly. He dragged him to Auntie May's back door. They stood there drenched and covered in mud and smelt dreadfully.

Mark knocked loudly at the door. Auntie Mary opened the door. They all trooped into her living room.

Auntie Mary began, "where've you been? I was frantic with worry. I was worried sick you were lost in the old quarry tunnels." Somewhat begrudgingly she added, "thank you Mark for bringing him back."

She turned to Andy, "and you'd better get upstairs and get in the bath. I will deal with you later."

With head down, Andy slouched out of the room.

With some trepidation Mark said, "I think the problem we've here is Andy needs some excitement. I wonder if you would let him come with me to Nice on Thursday for a couple of days."

Auntie Mary thought for a moment. "What would Madge say? She would be very angry with me."

"Well it could be our secret. We've had our secrets in the past haven't we?"

Auntie Mary blushed and looked down.

"I could tell Madge later. You're right. Andy needs more excitement than happens round here. I would have been in a mess if he ran away whilst you were abroad. I was frightened to death Welfare would take him if they found out."

Mark was slightly enjoying his one-upmanship with Auntie Mary.

"So this will be another of our secrets." Mark delicately replied.

.

CHAPTER THIRTEEN

Suddenly, the old man swung violently off the road. He headed down a track into the forest. "I guess you don't want to see those cops," he said meaningfully.

Andy woke up bright and breezy on Wednesday morning. He leaped out of bed with alacrity. He dressed quickly and rushed downstairs. Auntie Mary was astonished when he gave her a huge hug.

"What's all this about?" she asked.

"I'm going to France, I'm going to France," he said in a sing song manner.

By now, Andy realised he must make the best of the situation. He also thought he better be bright with Auntie Mary or she might hand him over to the Welfare.

"That's where the French live," he said in a proud manner as if he discovered a new truth.

Auntie Mary laughed. It was good to hear her laugh. Even she was surprised to hear herself. Perhaps having Andy was doing her good.

Andy ate his breakfast exuberantly. He even helped Auntie Mary clear away the table and do the washing up. Perhaps having Auntie Mary was doing Andy good!

Andy shot out into the garden. He remembered his butterfly notebook. He noticed a Red Admiral sunbathe on one of the 'vanilla' flowers. It was mostly black; its upper wings had distinctive red bands and a pattern of white markings near the tips. There were red borders on the bottom half of the lower wings. As he made a record in his notebook he heard a Pssst.

Turning round he saw 'the gang.'

"Hi, fellows," he said warmly, (fellows being a generic term which included Maisie)

"We came a couple of days ago but you weren't here," said Sammy.

"I went out with my Dad. I wanted to see my Mum. But they won't let me. I don't know why they won't let me. She IS my Mum."

"You poor thing," said Maisie.

"I ran away yesterday morning to see my Mum but they caught me."

"You poor thing," Maisie repeated.

"My Dad's trying to stop me seeing my Mum by taking me to Nice in the South of France. Perhaps if I do it his way, I'll get to see my Mum. At least, I'll get a ride on an aeroplane."

"I think you'll like Nice," said Danny. He was normally the quiet twin. Recently, he learned about France at school. He filled in Andy, and the others, with some details.

He said Nice was a warm and sunny, crescent-shaped area, a seaport, between the Alps and the Italian Gulf of Genoa.

He explained how marauding Greeks came over from Marseilles to conquer local tribes some two thousand three hundred and fifty years previously. They called the city by the Greek word "Nike" meaning victory.

The Greeks were followed by the Romans who in turn were followed by the Turks. Others ruled the city, although France managed to capture and occupy it from time to time. Eventually, Italy ceded Nice to France in 1860.

He mentioned the Nice Carnival which was a very exciting and colourful time. Everywhere were loads of colourful lorry floats which processed along the Promenade des Anglais.

This was two wide carriageways separated by flower beds and palm trees which stretched for two and a half miles (four kilometres) along the waterfront.

Danny was beginning to sound like a walking encyclopaedia!

With a wicked look in his eye, his coup de grace.

"All the dishes they serve you will be full of tomatoes. They'll have lashings of olive oil and fresh garlic chopped up all over them."

"Ugh!" the others chorused.

"I like garlic," Danny proudly announced. He was about to go into all the benefits of garlic. One look at their faces and he decided not to bother.

Instead, he went on to tell them about Grasse which was North of Nice: the perfume centre of France. How they cultivated Jasmine and other flowers, as well as bitter orange blossom from which the perfumes were distilled.

By this time, the other two boys had switched off. Only Maisie was listening intently. There was slightly renewed interest when Danny told them the town was also known for its candied fruit.

Eventually, even Maisie had had enough.

"Danny stop going on like that. Can't you see we should be helping Andy?" She moved closer to Andy. "Can't you get out of going?"

"No, my Dad said Welfare would lock me up if I ran away again. I guess I'll have to make the best of a bad job."

"Doesn't your Dad tell you how your Mum is going on?" Maisie asked.

"No, he's not allowed to see her. Do you think she's going to die?"

Maisie lifted up her face. She gazed at Andy.

"Oh, Andy, don't think like that. If she's in hospital they'll get her better."

She turned to the others.

"I know how we can cheer Andy up. Let's go and look at the tunnel Andy's found."

Maisie grabbed hold of Andy's hand and pulled him along. They all ran through the wood to the lean-to.

Sammy arrived first. He pulled open the door. Andy pushed past him and ran across to the tarpaulin. He unhooked it and yanked it back. He lifted up the door in the floor. There in all its glory was the 'rabbit hole.'

All four of them stood on the edge and surveyed it with wonder.

The silence was broken with Danny exclaiming,

"Wow, it's truly terrific."

The others nodded in agreement. It was all they could have hoped – a secret tunnel.

They couldn't see very well down the tunnel. They wondered what to do.

Andy said, "I've got a small torch in my pocket."

This time he remembered not only to slip it into his trouser pocket before he came out, but to take the battery from his radio. He checked the battery on his Auntie Mary's battery checker. It was a handy device. You popped the battery in. It registered either no lights or up to four lights if it were perfect. This reached three lights.

The one thing he hadn't with him was the map. Auntie Mary discovered and confiscated it when she unpacked his rucksack after he ran away to see his Mum.

They all got down on their hands and knees. They peered into the hole. Andy flashed a light down the hole. As their eyes became more accustomed, they saw a ledge a few feet down. It was followed by a bend. Their view was blocked after that. Their eyes shone with excitement. They wondered what was beyond the bend.

"I'm dying to know what's beyond the bend, I'm going down," said Sammy.

"How can you do that?" Danny asked. "I've been on the first ledge and it seems a long way to the next. Even if we struggle to that ledge how will we get back up here?"

The boys continued to look down the hole. They wondered what to do and how they could get down it.

Maisie left the boys' side and searched the lean-to. She rummaged amongst some old cloths, cloches and garden tools.

"Hey boys," she exclaimed. "There's a strong rope here."

They all helped her pull it out. They saw it was attached to a hook in the floor.

Taking charge, Sammy threw the free end of the rope down the hole. He put his leg over the edge to descend.

Andy stopped him.

"It's my tunnel, I should go first. Anyway I'm the one with the torch."

The others murmured their agreement. Sammy stood back to let Andy go down.

Gently, he lowered himself to the ledge. From there, he shone his torch around. It all looked very similar to what he had experienced. About three feet down was another ledge. He went down to the next ledge. This time, when he looked down, he could see there was a passage-way.

"Are you OK?" shouted Maisie.

"Yes," replied Andy. His voice sounded rather hollow as it bounced off the tunnel walls. "Come on down."

Gradually, they all scrambled down until they were alongside Andy. Alongside was not quite the right word as there was not much space. It was more like a queue. Maisie, as usual, was at the back. As she was the smallest she could not see anything.

With some trepidation, Andy went forward. The others followed. The torch was not too bright. It only lit up a few yards in front of them.

The tunnel was narrow. It was uneven under their feet. They had to be careful they did not fall.

After a few minutes, Maisie began to get scared. "Don't you think we should go back?" she said with a slight quiver in her voice.

Actually, it was fairly unpleasant for Maisie. It was very dark at the back. She was unable to see where she was going. She held tightly onto Danny's coat tails and stumbled along.

"Don't be stupid," said Sammy. "We've only just started." Under his breath he mumbled, "trust a girl."

Suitably put down, Maisie kept quiet. Inside fear was gripping her.

After a while, they came to a division. Part of the tunnel went one way and the other part went another way.

"Now what?" said Sammy, who could see over Andy's shoulder.

"I suggest two of us go one way and two the other," said Danny.

The others howled him down.

"And who," said Sammy with a smirk on his face, "would have the torch?"

"Oh, I never thought about that," replied Danny, somewhat crestfallen.

"You never think about anything."

Danny lowered his head dejectedly. He always hated it when Sammy put him down. After all, he was only half an hour older than him!

"I propose we take the left tunnel first." Sammy took charge (as he usually did.) "When we've explored that tunnel, we can come back and take the right tunnel."

"I think we should take the right," said Danny. As usual he was overruled by Sammy.

"I think we should go home," squeaked Maisie who was having great difficulty in controlling her fear.

As usual, Sammy bullied everyone. He got his own way.

As they set off down the left tunnel, they little realised what they would find.

.

CHAPTER FOURTEEN

"Thanks, Mister," said Harry "perhaps we can do the same for you one day. I guess you won't believe it but we're innocent."

Norma Brent was in the Probation Service for some twenty five years. She was proud of their history based on volunteers helping people at Court. This led to a very good attitude on behalf of the officers.

She was unhappy when her division of the Probation Service became part of the newly formed Children and Family Court Advisory and Support Service: CAFCASS. It was typical of the Civil Service to get everything down to initials.

She carefully opened the new file on her large oak desk. At the moment, the file was quite thin. She knew they grew rapidly.

As she read, she was surprised to find the Judge allowed unsupervised contact. She was even more surprised he allowed overnight staying contact where there was a history of violence.

"Andy Appleyard aged eight," she read. Thankfully, there did not seem to be any violence against Andy himself. Norma knew an atmosphere of violence bred violence. As the phrase was "Like Father, like son."

When she first started in the Probation Service, she was speechless when she read educated people were violent. She thought they would know better. Now nothing shocked her. Violence seemed to touch all classes of people.

It did not take her very long to carefully read all the Court documents. As she read, a little niggle troubled her mind. Something did not add up. It did not fall into the usual pattern of cases involving violence which she had done.

This was a very long marriage of some twenty three years. The Father changed in the last two years. Perhaps, when she talked to the Mother and Father and with Andy she might get a better picture.

She had a large case load. She wondered when she could see the Appleyards.

She preferred to see them in their own home rather than in the office. She made a better assessment of them when they were in their own environment. She considered it important to see how the children related with their parents in their own home.

Usually, she spent a short time with the family together. After a while, she sent the parents out of the room on a pre-arranged pretext. This way, she saw the children in the absence of their parents.

It was surprising how much the children would open up to her. Perhaps, they appreciated her comfortable and easy going manner.

She found out a lot about the family and family dynamics in these sessions.

It amazed her how intensely loyal the children were to their parents, even in cases were they were beaten by their parent or where one of the parents was an alcoholic or drug abuser.

She visited some homes where the awful smell enveloped her. Some homes were so poor the children had old raincoats or coats on their beds instead of blankets. The younger children ran around naked. The children loved their parents. They did not realise their poverty was due to their parents drinking.

If the children sided strongly with one parent as against the other, she became suspicious of undue influencing by the other parent. This caused her great concern. A problem she found difficult to solve. She realised, as time went on, the problem usually escalated. In the end, the children said they would not visit the other parent. They would not know why or would parody an explanation given by their parent.

She spent about an hour with the family on the first occasion. She went back for a slightly longer session the second time.

As the parents were usually separated, she arranged for the children to visit each home in turn. This way, she saw the children with each parent. This was sometimes difficult to arrange when the parents were workers or lived a long way away.

She felt the burden of the huge responsibility of her work. She realised the Judges laid great store by what she wrote and said. In nearly every case, the Court followed her recommendation.

Norma leafed through the file. Inside, she found a page of information about the parents: their address and their telephone number. She thought she would ring Madge first at Auntie Mary's and try and fix an appointment with her.

She dialled Auntie Mary's telephone number. She let it ring quite a long time but there was no reply. She dialled Mark next: no reply. Sometimes her work was very frustrating!

She closed the file and walked over to the filing cabinet. She retrieved another file and began to read.

A knock at the door, it was Susie. Susie was a post graduate student at the University. Her course involved her spending eight weeks with the Probation Service and with CAFCASS. At the end of her assignment she had to write a long dissertation on the two services in which she discussed what impact changes had on the services.

Susie was enjoying her time with CAFCASS. She found Norma very helpful.

Norma had an old-fashioned three wheeler car which Norma called Robina. They piled into it when they went out visiting clients. The seats were very low in the car. They could hardly see out of the front windscreen. The car was very old. Susie was surprised it had even passed its MOT test of road worthiness. Anyway, it always started up and they arrived – what more could you ask from a car.

Susie found Norma to be very conscientious. She often arranged to meet clients after work hours or even at the week-end.

Yesterday, they visited Mrs. Ranter and her family. The

Ranters had six children who loved their Mum very much. None of them wanted to see their Dad. In this case, Norma considered their reasons were genuine. The case had all the hallmarks of abuse by the Dad. The Dad repeatedly beat up his wife.

Before they left the CAFCASS office, Norma warned Susie to put some perfume on her inner wrist. If the smell became too bad she should keep taking a whiff! They managed to last out an hour. Afterwards, they sat in the car for a while whilst Norma painstakingly wrote up her notes of the interview.

Today, Norma was busy catching up on her paperwork. Norma looked up when Susie came in.

"Hi, Norma, are we going out this afternoon?" She loved going out on what she called field trips.

"No," said Norma. "I've arranged for Mr. Ranter to visit the office today. I want to talk with him at length before I arrange for an interview when the children are present."

Susie was surprised to hear this because Norma always went out to the clients' home.

"Why are you having Mr. Ranter coming to the office instead of visiting him in his home?" Susie enquired.

"Mrs. Ranter and indeed the children have made some very serious allegations of abuse. I want to interview him on our territory in case anything goes wrong. At least in the office there're people about if I need help."

Although she realised it was a very interesting and varied profession, it was dawning on Susie there were sometimes dangers in being a CAFCASS officer.

"Also," continued Norma. "I want to be sure he is sufficiently committed to come and see me as opposed to my going out to see him. I suspect he won't even arrive at the office."

From time to time, Norma met people like Mr. Ranter. She found they made an enormous fuss at Court. When it came to actually being involved with the children, they failed to turn up for contact.

This, she knew, was very damaging to the children as they looked forward to their Dad coming. They were very disappointed when he did not arrive. They felt their Dad had abandoned or rejected them. This made it much harder for them to trust other people when they became older.

Even as they spoke, the door burst open. Mr. Ranter exploded into the room. "What's going on? What's this about my wife saying, I've hurt the kids? I'm no paedophile."

"Calm down Mr. Ranter and sit down," said Norma quietly.

"I won't sit down. Why's she saying all this rubbish about me?" Mr. Ranter went over to Norma's desk. He leaned over her in a menacing way. He poked his finger in her face.

"What are you going to do about it?"

"Mr. Ranter for the last time, will you sit down."

"There's no way I'm going to sit in your office. You're all the same, you women, ganging up together. Well, I tell you, you haven't heard the last of me," he shouted.

Norma quietly murmured to herself. "I'm sure I haven't."

"What did you say?" asked Mr. Ranter.

"I said good afternoon."

Mr. Ranter paused for a second, "who said I was going? You've not heard my side."

Surreptitiously, Norma pressed a panic button. Almost immediately, two men came in.

Mr. Ranter said, "thank goodness I can tell my side to a man."

The two security men told him they were escorting him from the premises.

"What! I want to have my say," Mr. Ranter shouted. He was still shouting and ranting as the two men forcibly removed him from the room.

"Phew, that was nasty," said Susie "I can see why you wanted him to come to the office."

"Well," said Norma, "it takes allsorts."

"Has anything new come in?" Susie asked.

Briefly, Norma told Susie about the Appleyard case. She explained she was unable to make contact with the parents.

"I find it very curious the Father only become violent in the last two years," said Susie. "Do you think he has a medical problem, something awful like a brain tumour?"

"Can you get the Court to order a medical investigation?" Asked Susie

"Yes," answered Norma. "All this will have to be investigated and I might well ask the Court for a medical report. "

There was a whirring noise in the corner as the fax machine sprung into life. Norma walked across to the machine. She waited for a minute or two for the machine to spew out its contents. She picked up the letter from the Court. Norma let out a slight gasp as she read about Madge's accident. The case was beginning to take on a real urgency.

CHAPTER FIFTEEN

"No, I don't believe you're innocent," said the old man. He pulled a gun on them. "I want to make sure I get any reward that's going."

"I'm tired of trudging down this horrid dark tunnel," announced Maisie. Tears rolled down her thin, worried face. They left a trail of a long, dirty stain on her face. She kept rubbing her dirty hands across her eyes which made the smudges worse. To tell you the truth, she was more than a little scared. They seemed to have been down the tunnel for a very long time. She was glad of the darkness so the others could not see her crying. She reckoned without Andy.

He suddenly turned round. He shone the torch full in her face. As soon as they saw her red-rimmed eyes and heard her stifled sobbing, they cried out almost in unison.

"You cry baby."

As her sobbing grew louder, they took pity on her.

"I tell you what," said Andy, "let's go round the next corner and then go home."

At that Maisie brightened up and managed a weak smile.

As they turned the next corner, they bumped into each other, like a set of dominoes falling down, as the tunnel ended in a solid wall.

A huge look of disappointment showed on everyone's face.

For a brief moment, there was silence broken by Danny murmuring, "I told you we should take the right tunnel."

Thankfully, Sammy did not hear what he said or there would have been ructions.

"Can we go back now?" whined Maisie.

"Oh shut up," replied Sammy, "it's just like a girl to whine."

"No it isn't."

"Yes it is."

"No, it is not."

"Come on you two," said Andy, "cut it out, we're not going anywhere by you're arguing."

"This doesn't make sense," Andy continued, "why would anyone dig out a tunnel for about a mile with loads of bends and come to an abrupt halt?"

He looked round. He shone his torch on the wall in front of him. The light made shadows as he manipulated the torch. He shone it on the wall on either sides of the end of the tunnel. This was followed by him shining it round the floor. Finally, he shone it up on the roof. The shaft of light went higher and higher as he did so.

All the gang breathlessly followed the beam of his torch with their eyes.

"Look!" he said, "look, up there. Can you see there's a ledge? Look, part way up, it looks like the one we had when we came down," he excitedly shouted.

His torch lingered on the ledge so everyone could see it clearly.

"Now what do we do?" said Danny, "there's no way we can climb up there."

"I guess one of us will have to climb onto the shoulders of another," said Sammy.

"Maisie is the lightest. I propose Maisie gets on your shoulders, Sammy, and climbs up and looks," Andy replied.

Maisie was not sure she wanted to do this. However, the thought of trudging the entire journey back underground boosted her confidence.

Carefully, Andy and Danny helped Maisie onto Sammy's shoulders.

Although she only looked a wisp of a thing, Sammy was surprised how heavy she was.

With great circumspection, she balanced on his shoulders. She straightened up. Warily ran her hands over the floor of the ledge. As she did so, something whizzed past her face. It fell in a crumpled heap onto the floor.

Maisie let out a piercing scream. With the shock of it Sammy jumped. Maisie fell off his shoulders and landed next to the object.

The boys looked on with shock at Maize's curled up body. They did not know whether to help Maisie or to see what was on the floor.

Good manners and gallantry prevailed. In reality they had a concern for Maize's welfare. They helped her to her feet.

"Ouch," she said as she tried to stand. "I've really hurt my ankle."

Andy shone the torch. The light played on the bundle on the floor.

"Why," he exclaimed, "it's a thick tow rope." As he flashed his torch on it, he saw part of it was still extending beyond the ledge.

"It looks as if it's used as a means of escape," said Danny.

They um'd and ah'd what to do next and who should go first.

Sammy, somewhat bravely, volunteered to go first. As he cagily climbed up the rope, he was secretly concerned as to what he might find.

With much perseverance and struggling, he clambered onto the shelf.

He had the presence of mind to take the torch from Andy. He flashed the light carefully up the wall. Another shelf was above him. Although it lower than the first shelf, he was too small to reach it.

"Can you send Maisie?" he called down, "she can see if there's another rope up here."

Maisie was very reluctant to go up again into the great unknown, particularly as her ankle was throbbing like mad. However the thought of staying down in this tunnel any longer than necessary provoked her to go up again.

This time she used the rope. She was actually quite good at climbing ropes. She won prizes at school for being the fastest in her class to climb a rope. But doing this underground was a different kettle of fish. With some difficulty and a great deal of nervousness, Maisie climbed up the rope.

"If I kneel down," Sammy said to her, "you can scramble onto my back and see if you can reach as far as the next shelf."

Even he, with all his cockiness, was becoming apprehensive about their situation. He felt very insecure on this tiny shelf.

Maisie managed to mount onto Sammy's back. She stretched as high as she could but was unable to stretch far enough. Although she could touch the shelf, she was about an inch too short to reach over the ledge.

Now they had a problem, as the shelf they were on was very narrow. It was barely wide enough for two of them.

Maisie could not believe it. She was so near to getting out of the tunnel and she was too short to reach the ledge.

Somewhat begrudgingly, Maisie descended. She would rather go down the rope than have one of the boys standing on her back.

As Andy was the tallest he volunteered to go up next. When he reached the ledge he scrambled onto Sammy's back. He carefully ran his hand over the ledge. The trick was to find the rope, without the rope knocking them both down from the ledge.

Yes, the rope was there. This time it seemed a much thinner rope. Andy cautiously curled his hand round it. He grasped it tightly. He was able to pull it gradually down.

Andy climbed up the rope with the torch between his teeth.

As he was nearly on the next ledge he shone the torch upwards.

The roof was only a few feet above him. The distance between the ledge and the roof was about three feet so he could not fully stand upright.

Meanwhile, Sammy straightened up what was now his aching back. It was not used to human weight on it.

He called out, "what can you see? Is there anything up there?"

"I can only see a ceiling," replied Andy. "I can't see any way out."

"Oh, no!" squealed Maisie, "I'm going to suffocate. I'm going to die down here."

"Don't be silly;" shouted Sammy, "we can always go back the way we came."

"Oh, no, I can't go back, I can't go back," exclaimed Maisie in a high soprano voice. "I know we're going to die, I know we're going to die. I just know it." The pitch of her voice was getting higher and higher.

"You're all we need," said Sammy, "a girl moaning on, and on and on. "Mona, Mona Lisa," he chanted, as if he were in the school playground.

"Oh. Stop it you two," called down Andy, "I can't concentrate with all your carping."

By this time, he was gently running his free hand along the ceiling whilst he pointed the torch with the other.

A slow smile crept along his face. He realised there was a thin rectangular crack line on the ceiling.

Gingerly, he pushed at the roof. It gave way. A hinge like flap fell open and there was daylight.

He stood up on the ledge, looked around and could not believe his eyes.

CHAPTER SIXTEEN

There was a struggle, a shot rang out. The old man fell back. Fortunately, he was not too badly hurt. Pete and Harry tied him up and escaped in his car.

Madge opened her eyes and groaned. She was feeling a bit better but with the improvement came the sense of pain. Every bone in her body ached.

All the equipment and tubes were removed. She was able to sit up and look around.

Sitting on chairs at the bottom of her bed were Nurse Phillips and another lady. The two of them were talking quietly together.

The lady was in her mid forties. She seemed to be about five feet five inches tall, with closely cropped mousy hair. She was dressed in a dark suit. In her hand, she held a bundle of papers.

There was a slight pause in the conversation. Nurse Phillips turned to Madge.

114

"This is Norma Brent. She is the CAFCASS officer."

As Madge looked all at sea, Norma took control of the situation.

"You may remember you were at Court recently. You wanted a Residence Order for your son Andy? Well, the Court has asked me to come along and interview you."

Norma told Madge how she had spoken with Doctor Tinsley at some length. He told her about the remarkable progress Madge was making. They expected her to go home in a few weeks time.

Norma described what CAFCASS was and what her role was, vis a vis, the Court.

She outlined the part she played. She explained she was required to speak with the Mother and the Father and with Andy to get something of the background of the case. She explained the Court regarded the welfare of Andy as priority.

Norma nodded her head. She was finding it a little difficult to take it all in. What had not escaped her was she was going home in a few weeks time. Secretly, she was very pleased about this, although it would seem forever.

Norma continued to tell her the role of CAFCASS was to be the ears and eyes of the Court. She interviewed the people either in person or by telephone.

She contacted the school, any witnesses and possibly anyone the parents wanted her to speak to. She checked with the Police and the medical profession to ensure there were no problems there.

She explained it was good practice to see the parents in their own home. She would watch how Andy related to his parents.

She told Madge she needed to see Andy on his own. She explained how she did this. She gathered everyone in the room together. After a short while, she made some pretext for the relevant parent to go out of the room. This way she could talk with Andy by himself.

"But first," Norma said, "I want you to tell me what has been happening. Why did you go to the Court? Just take your time."

As tears ran down Madge's face, Norma hastily added, "don't worry, I'll come back another day."

"No, no, it's alright to discuss the matter with you whilst I'm here in hospital."

Not only did Madge hope it would speed matters along but she was beginning to get very bored with being in hospital.

Slowly, the story unfolded. Madge told of how she and Mark married some twenty three years earlier.

At first, they had a carefree existence. They went out when they wanted. A couple of nights a week they went out with friends. They went on exotic holidays twice a year. They visited places like Thailand and New Zealand.

They always seemed to have money in their pocket as they were both working in those days. They bought what they wanted when they wanted.

A baby came: Patsy. Things changed overnight. Patsy cried a lot with colic. Madge and Mark had many a broken night, with one or other of them getting up in the night to see to Patsy.

Madge gave up her job to look after Patsy full time. Money became very tight. It did not seem to go anywhere with having to buy nappies and everything else a young baby needed.

One evening, they had a family conference. They decided Madge would have to get a job. Madge's Mum offered to help with Patsy. This allowed Madge to go to work.

Madge found this increasingly difficult. She was very tired when she returned after a day's hard work. She had all the housework to do and see to Patsy as well.

After a while, they got into a routine. Madge told Norma what a tremendous help Mark was. He was a wonderful Father. Nothing seemed too much trouble.

He lent a hand with getting meals and with bathing Patsy. He assisted in putting her to bed. After tucking her up, he read to her. He still got up in the night although this was not very often by then.

They went through what all the books called the 'terrible two's' when Patsy had the screaming abdabs. In the middle of the supermarket, she threw herself on the floor in a tantrum.

This was followed by the "troublesome threes." At five, Patsy was old enough to go to school.

Came that terrible day when Patsy was nine. Soon after she returned from school she complained of feeling very hot.

Madge felt her and was surprised to find her hands and feet were very cold. She started to complain about her head hurting too much. She vomited. She breathed rapidly. Madge was concerned about meningitis.

She and Mark talked it over and decided to take her to Accident and Emergency at the local hospital.

She remembered the Doctor saying, "yes, she has meningitis. I'm glad you didn't wait for a rash. I think we can save her."

The night passed very slowly and Patsy seemed to be brightening up.

About seven in the evening, Patsy sat up and held out her arms. As Madge picked her up and cuddled her, she died.

Madge was overwhelmed with grief. She was inconsolable. Heartbroken was not in it. They were absolutely devastated. Their lovely, darling Patsy was no longer there.

Madge wandered round their home in a daze. She left Patsy's bedroom as it was the day she died. She went into it regularly.

She put her pyjamas against her face and kept deeply smelling Patsy. She sobbed and sobbed.

They talked about having another baby. Madge knew Mark always wanted a boy. Not just to carry on the family name but someone with whom he could play football after work. Someone he could take swimming on a Saturday.

Mark was over the moon when Andy was born.

Their life became restricted but Mark certainly pulled his weight. He helped in every way he could. He shared equally with the care of Andy.

As Madge was recounting this history, her vivid blue eyes were lighting up from time to time with the joy of what she was remembering. Her voice was light and vibrant.

"What went wrong?" Norma gently asked.

Madge's face clouded over. The earlier exuberance faded as she continued her story.

"About two years ago, Mark started a new job at a chemical factory. It was a fabulous job with Mark doing highly secretive work in the laboratory. He gave lectures in different parts of the world. He received twice as much as in his previous job. Sometimes, he was allowed to take me abroad with him." She paused to take a breath.

"After that Mark began to change. He became increasingly irritable and cantankerous. On the occasions I went out of the country with him, it turned out to be a nightmare rather than a pleasure. I usually regretted going with him."

I realised he had to do long hours. I know he was doing a great amount of travelling but his personality seemed to change.

He wasn't the man I married. He wasn't the Father I'd seen."

Madge went on to tell how lately he started rows. These were usually over a pretext.

He came home from work, went to the bedroom. He came down at tea-time. He expected Madge to have prepared and cooked the tea. If it were a few minutes late, he flew into a temper. After tea he went back upstairs for hours on end. If she went upstairs to find out what was wrong, he shouted and yelled at her.

Lately, he started to throw things. Plates were his favourite. The plates smashed on the floor and broke into smithereens. He bawled at her until she swept up the last tiny piece.

The final straw was that petrifying car ride and when he hit her. She left with Andy and ran away to a flat. Things proved too expensive for her so they went to stay at Auntie Mary's.

By now a trickle of tears was making a path down Madge's face.

Norma was tempted to stop the conversation there and then. But she needed one more piece of information.

"Did Andy see any of this?"

"Yes that was the worst part. Andy couldn't understand why his Dad was like this. He never threw anything at Andy or hit him."

She paused slightly before continuing "I don't want to see Mark at all. He's going worse. Where will it all lead?"

"There, there," said Norma, "I think we've talked enough for one day. I'll come again next week to visit you. Hopefully I'll see Mark in the meantime."

Raising her voice defiantly Madge added, "You mustn't let him see Andy. Mark is dangerous, highly dangerous."

Madge lay down after Norma left. She was semi-asleep when the door opened and Mark came in.

Very lovingly, Mark whispered, "Madge, Madge."

With a welcoming but drowsy voice, Madge replied, "hello." She stirred and opened her eyes.

On seeing Mark, her eyes filled with fear. "What are you doing here?"

"Madge, love, I couldn't stay away whilst you were so poorly." Mark gently replied.

"I don't need you. Get out." She struggled to sit up.

"Can't we try again, even if it is only for Andy's sake?"

"No, Mark, it's all over."

"I don't know what's been getting into me lately. I seem to be so on edge all the time," he admitted.

"You should have done something about it before now. You're too late."

"Madge, darling, you know I love you."

"Actions speak louder than words."

Mark moved towards her as if he would put his arm round her. His eyes were full of tenderness and love.

"Oh, Madge, I've missed you so much."

"And I've missed all your bawling and violence."

"Madge, I'll change."

"If you meant that, you would have changed before. I don't believe you."

"Just give me one more chance."

"You've had your chances. Just go – now."

By now, Madge was getting more and more agitated.

Summoning up all her strength she shouted, "get out, get out." She turned in bed so her back was toward Mark.

Mark walked round the bed to face her.

"Madge, won't you listen to me. I love you very much. I want you and Andy home."

"All you care about is yourself." With a huge effort and with a great deal of pain, Madge pulled herself up.

"Get out or I'll call the Police."

Madge leaned across to the cupboard by her bed. Her hand waived uncertainly toward her bell. It was just out of reach. She turned toward Mark. Her fists were going up and down with rage.

"Get out, get out, get out, get out," she screamed.

She reached again to the cupboard by her bed. She grasped her glass tumbler of water. With all the power she could muster, she threw it at Mark. It narrowly missed him. It shattered into thousands of pieces on the floor.

Madge struggled to get out of bed. She pulled back the bedclothes, manoeuvred her legs over the side of the bed. She tried to stand but her poorly legs would not take the weight. She fell by the broken glass on the floor.

Mark rushed to her side and tried to lift her up. She clawed his face and drew blood as he tried to get her back into bed.

Nurse Phillips heard the commotion in the corridor and rushed in.

"Get him out of here, get him out of here," Madge screamed.

As Nurse Phillips turned to face Mark he said, "it's alright I'm leaving." With that he walked out.

A look of consternation shot across Nurse Phillips face as she saw the distress Madge was in.

Nurse Phillips opened the door. She called for help. Two other nurses rushed in. They gently picked Madge up from the floor.

Madge was greatly agitated. She kept flaying her arms about. Nurse Phillips had great difficulty in inserting a syringe into Madge. The other two nurses held Madge firmly. Gradually as the drug worked, she relaxed and passed out.

CHAPTER SEVENTEEN

"Now we've torn it," said Pete, "if the old geezer dies we'll be on a murder rap; as if we're not in enough trouble already."

The taxi pulled up at the airport. Andy opened the door and jumped out. He could see some of the airplanes stationary on the ground.

Although he knew it was a trick to get him away from seeing his Mum, he was pleased to be flying on a plane and with his Dad.

They walked into the large waiting area. Opposite the entrance were outsized boards on the wall giving details of various flight times. In front of the boards were barriers through which people passed. These were manned by airport staff in uniform. Around the waiting room were a number of small shops and kiosks.

He and his Dad meandered around for a while. They wandered in and out of the various shops.

Andy bought a post card for his Mum and posted it. He wondered how long it would be before he saw his Mum.

They bought stationery with the airport emblem on it.

Occasionally, the thought of what he saw when he looked out of the tunnel flashed through his mind. The large aircraft hangar type building: the two men. Their countenance was evil personified. He had never seen such wicked looking men. It worried him.

He decided to try and put it all out of his mind, enjoy the airport and the prospect of flying.

A voice boomed out of loudspeakers round the entrance hall. They announced changes in flight time. Andy started when he heard their flight number. The announcement told them the plane was delayed half an hour. Andy was happy about this. It gave him time to watch other planes landing and taking off. Large planes, small planes left the runways. He wondered how they were able to be so precise and meticulous about the timing especially as there were frequent changes in flight time.

"Dad," said Andy, "can we go and see the control room?"

"No, we haven't time. However I've a friend who works in there. I'm sure when we come back, I can arrange for us to have a full tour of the airport."

Andy was overjoyed at this prospect. He sure would have loads to tell his mates when he got back to school.

The time sped by very quickly. They went through checkout or rather check in. They took all the metal, including coins and keys, out of their pockets before they walked through an archway. The man at the barrier asked them to hand up their shoes for inspection.

As Andy went through the barrier, there was a loud bleep.

The official took a short baton and waved it round Andy's body. He was a bit embarrassed when the official asked him to check his pockets again. The culprit was revealed. It was a metal marble which he treasured. He had won it from a school friend. The man waved the baton over and round Andy again. All was clear.

They watched as their entire luggage, laid on a conveyor belt, disappeared into a tunnel. Mark and Andy carried a small bag each.

They walked leisurely across the concourse toward their plane. Andy saw luggage going into a large opening on the side of the plane.

A long staircase went up to another opening. This was situated quite a way up the side of the plane. Andy had seen these steps before on television but not realised how huge they were.

Two airhostesses stood at the top of the stairs. His Dad took their tickets out of his pocket and showed them to the airhostesses. They were waved onto the plane.

They had a super seat by the window Andy glanced out of the window. He saw two men talking to an official at the bottom of the gangway.

"Surely they can't be?" Andy said to himself. He thought he must be dreaming. But they really looked like the two men he saw at the end of the tunnel.

"Don't be silly, why would they be going to Nice?"

As the two men mounted the gangway, he tried to get a better look but their heads were turned away from Andy.

He could not see them properly.

He looked in another direction. A motorised truck coming to the plane carried two ladies in it. He later overheard them talking. He realised they missed the last call for the plane. Indeed, they nearly missed the plane itself.

They closed the plane's door with a big bang. A rattle of metal as the staircase was moved.

The announcement came over the tannoy, "please fasten your seatbelts we are about to take off."

Andy looked round to see if he could see the two men but the backs of the seats were far too high for him to look over.

The engines made a huge whirring sound as they kicked into life. The airplane barely moved along the runway before its nose went sharply into the air. They were airborne.

Gradually, they climbed higher and higher. Houses shrunk. Cars dwarfed into toy cars. People and sheep were little moving dots on the landscape.

As they moved above the clouds, Andy was taken aback to find it was a sunny day up there. He was happy to leave the wet English weather behind.

A loud announcement came over the loudspeaker system, "you may unfasten your seat belts now."

Andy was dying to see if he could see the men.

"Excuse me, Dad. I must go to the toilet."

He pushed past Mark and slowly walked to the back of the plane. As he walked down the central aisle, he carefully looked at all the passengers. It was clear they were not at the back of the plane. If they were on the plane they must be in front of him. There was no way he could go that way.

He arrived back at his seat as the airhostess came round with a large tray containing a selection of food.

Despite feeling sick, he pushed down the sausage and chips followed by ice-cream.

His Dad gave him a tablet before they set off to make sure he was not air sick.

Gradually, Andy felt very sleepy. Soon he was fast asleep.

He woke with a start when his Dad shook him, "we're here, Andy."

He looked up. He remembered the two men and watched as people walked past him. Unfortunately, some passengers had already passed him before he woke up.

They descended from the plane and walked across the tarmac at Nice airport.

It was a warm, sultry day. Next, they went through Customs.

The Customs Officers required them to open up their bags and they rummaged inside. They showed their passports.

When he was little he had to be on his Dad's passport. Now he was allowed his own passport. This really pleased Andy.

That marble again caused some problems. Eventually, Customs let them through.

They came out to the taxi rank just as a taxi was pulling away. Andy did a double take - he could have sworn the two men were in it.

"Hotel d"Europe," said Mark to a taxi driver.

It was quite a shock to Andy to find they drove on the wrong side of the road. They called it the right. Well, I guess it was the right as opposed to the left side of the road. As far as Andy was concerned, it was not the right, it was the wrong side of the road.

Mark turned to Andy, "This is the Promenade des Anglais which means English Promenade. It runs all along the front of Nice alongside the sea."

Andy was a bit disappointed. It did not really look like Blackpool. Where was the funfair? Where were the amusement arcades? Where was the beach? All he could see was shingles where the sand should have been.

"Tomorrow," Mark continued, "we will hardly be able to walk along here, never mind drive along, as there'll be a huge Carnival."

At this Andy brightened up.

The taxi drew up outside a hotel with a canopy over the entrance. They went into the hotel and booked in at reception. They went up to their room on the fifth floor.

Their room was en suite with two single beds.

They unpacked. They had a quick brush up and went out into the town.

They walked for a few minutes along the Promenade des Anglais and turned inland down a side street.

"I know a café down here," said Mark, "where the food is really good."

"Here it is." He stopped outside a café with a number of tables outside, Gaudy, brightly coloured umbrellas gave protection from the sun. Mark walked up to the window to read what was on the menu.

As his Dad read the menu, Andy went to look into the café. He glanced at the window and saw, reflected through the café window, two men. They looked like the two men he saw from the tunnel. He quickly turned round but they disappeared.

"What was going on?" he wondered.

CHAPTER EIGHTEEN

"What else could we do?" asked Harry,
"we couldn't let him hand us in."

Madge was feeling a little better. It was easier sitting up in bed. She appreciated the summer sunshine streaming in through her window. Nonchalantly, she flicked through a magazine. She settled down to read the short story. She was startled by a knock at her door.

Auntie Mary walked in, laden with wild flowers from her garden.

"Hello, Madge, They wouldn't let me come before," said Auntie Mary gruffly. "How are you feeling?"

"Things are getting better. They say I can go home in a few weeks time. But how is Andy."

Auntie Mary replied somewhat cagily, "just fine. You'd never believe how much he's changed. He's even helping clear the table."

"Why didn't you bring him?" Madge demanded.

"Er, the hospital wouldn't let him come, so I left him, er," she rushed on to add. "He's made good friends with some local children. He's spending a lot of time with them these days."

Auntie Mary tried to change the subject.

"I was walking along the edge of the rec. (recreational ground) yesterday when I saw a kingfisher dive into the pond. I was very excited as this was the first time..."

Madge interrupted her, "you're not listening. I need to see Andy. Mary, I need your help. Mark mustn't get to see Andy."

"But he's his Dad," Auntie Mary exclaimed.

Somewhat impatiently Madge replied, "No, listen! I've a plan and you must help me until we've our own home again."

"Well, if I can."

"I've decided to appear as helpful as possible over Andy seeing his Dad. But every time he should see him, I'll think up an excuse so it doesn't happen. I'll ring the solicitors at the last moment. I'll say he's ill or he's got a party. I'll think of something."

"But won't Andy be upset when his Dad doesn't turn up?"

"No, this is the clever part of my plan. We've to keep telling Andy he's the man of the house. We've to get distressed every time Mark's name is mentioned. I'll tell Andy all the bad things which have happened in the marriage. The best part of all is we'll tell Andy his Dad hasn't bothered to come."

"What if he writes or phones?" Auntie Mary wanted to know.

"That's where you've to help me the most, by making sure one of us answers the phone and to watch out for the post in the morning."

Auntie Mary looked hard and long at Madge.

"You're out of your mind. What will you achieve by this? If the authorities find out they'll take Andy away from you. They'll say the accident has caused psychiatric damage."

"They won't find out if you help me. I've got to get Andy to tell the Court Reporter he doesn't want to see Mark. I've very little time to turn him against his Dad."

"Why are you going to all this trouble?" asked Auntie Mary. "I never thought I'd be arguing Mark's corner but Andy loves his Dad."

Madge ran her hand through her hair.

"I know but I don't trust Mark. He's a danger to Andy."

"What proof have you he'd hurt Andy?" asked Auntie Mary.

By now, Madge was getting agitated and upset.

"Are you calling me a liar? So, you're taking Mark's side now: what's with you and Mark?"

"Oh, Madge love. I'm your sister, remember," said Auntie Mary with uncustomary tenderness.

"I tell you Mark's dangerous," said Madge, Her voice rose in fear.

"But," began Auntie Mary.

Madge interrupted, "there's no but. You're either my sister or you're not. You've to choose."

"You thought I was wonderful once," said Auntie Mary quietly and pointedly.

Madge went very silent.

.

CHAPTER NINETEEN

"We need to buy time so we can prove we're innocent," said Pete. "The old geezer would have wrecked everything."

Maisie was surprised how quickly she recovered from the last ordeal of going down the tunnel.

After Andy looked out and saw the two evil looking men and the large aeroplane hangar, he shot back down from the ledge. He told them all he saw.

They held a pow-wow. After conferring, even Maisie agreed the only way out was to make the painful return journey along the tunnel and exit by their original entrance.

Today, Maisie and the twins came round to find Andy. When they arrived in his garden, they remembered he had gone to France. They discussed the tunnel. It seemed such a long time before Andy would be back.

Sammy was the keenest to go and have another look. To be honest, he had dreamed about nothing else since they arrived at home.

135

"Come on," Sammy boldly said, "let's go and look down the other tunnel."

"I don't think we should," replied Maisie emphatically. "It's Andy's tunnel. Anyway we haven't got a torch."

"Yes, we have," said Sammy triumphantly, as he pulled a grand looking torch from an inside pocket in his raincoat.

"Well, I still don't think we should go down without Andy."

"Trust girls," said Sammy, "they're always so frightened."

"No I'm not," said Maisie. With her heart pounding so loudly she thought the twins would hear it, she marched purposefully through the wood. When she reached the lean-to, she dragged open the door, pulled back the tarpaulin and lifted the lid.

Carefully, the three of them clambered onto the ledges until they were into the tunnel. They set off on their long march through the cold, dark tunnel until they came to the crossroads.

This time there was no decision making. They all knew it was the right hand tunnel which had to be investigated.

The way along the right tunnel was harder than the left tunnel. They kept feeling bumps like pieces of metal under their feet. They steadfastly plodded on in a silence which was occasionally punctuated with an "ow" or "that hurt."

Although they were getting used to tunnel travel, the right side seemed to have more bends than the left one. Occasionally, they knocked their arms on the side.

As they came round a corner, they came to an abrupt halt. Like the left tunnel, the tunnel ended with a blank wall in front of them.

Of course, by now they knew what to do. Sammy immediately lifted his torch so the light played near the ceiling. To their surprise, there was no ledge.

"Oh, we've walked miles for nothing," complained Maise.

"I don't think that can be right," said Danny.

He was the brainiest of the three.

"Why would someone go to all this trouble to dig out a long, twisting tunnel to end with a blank wall?"

"Perhaps they hadn't finished digging it out," Maisie suggested helpfully.

"Don't be silly;" said Sammy, "we would see evidence of their digging into a bit of the wall."

Whilst the two of them were bickering, Danny took the torch from Sammy. He looked on the floor.

"Look," he said, "they're some bits of metal on the floor near the corner."

He bent down and ran his hand into the corner. He felt a sharp metal piece sticking out and shifted it sideways.

Suddenly, the wall opened up.

In front of them was a huge cave.

Inside, it was all the appearance of a work shed with benches and tools. Besides a number of tiny scales were glass instruments.

They looked as if they had walked into their chemistry laboratory at school.

Lying about were a number of small machines which all looked identical. They were about two feet by eighteen inches in size. Principally, they looked like a gyroscope with rotating blades underneath.

The children were later to learn more detail. This was a rotating superconductor. Apparently, these gyros were made of brass, aluminium and silicon steel. They were able to spin at twenty thousand revs per minute. If you looked from above, they spun clockwise. This enabled lift off.

Round the blades was a shield, which emitted a high frequency magnetic field. These were time-varying magnets. Round the shield was a bag which contained liquid nitrogen and mercury mixed. The level of the mix was vital.

Beneath the shield was a small container. The machines had lightweight strong straps which gave the appearance as if they were satchels to be worn on the back. The sort the children had only ever seen in James Bond films.

As they stared with wide open mouths, they heard a sound behind them.

"Quick," said Maisie, "the wall's closing."

With great alacrity, they fled out of the cave. They were only just in time as the wall closed.

The children tumbled in a heap on the floor in the tunnel. Their hearts were beating like mad.

"That was a close thing," said Maisie shaking with fear.

They disentangled themselves, scrambled to their feet, stood and looked at each other.

The first one to break the silence was Danny.

"Wow, wait till we tell Andy."

"I don't think we should tell Andy," said Sammy, who was beginning to feel a bit guilty. "I think we should come with him as if we don't know what is here."

The others two were also feeling a bit guilty. They readily agreed.

The three of them set off down the tunnel on their way back. They chatted about what they had seen. The contents of the cave and the machines were quite a puzzle to them. They realised they were very expensive. They must have a very important task to do.

The journey back did not seem so long. They were soon back by the entrance. Danny went up the rope first and pushed at the lid. It was fast, solid. He pushed again but nothing happened. With ashen face, he climbed down the rope to the other two and explained.

"Don't be silly," said Sammy, "you're not strong enough, I should have gone first."

He climbed the rope. He pushed with all his might and nothing happened.

Maisie screamed.

"We're trapped for ever."

.

CHAPTER TWENTY

They tore along the narrow lanes which went through the forest until they bounced onto the highway. Turning right, they set off on their long journey to California.

A lovely sunny morning, Madge was sitting up in bed. She was dressed in a pretty pink nightdress with a matching pink bed jacket. She had a shower. Everything felt fresh and clean. The hairdresser called the previous day and did her hair. She felt a lot brighter. Her energy was returning.

She enjoyed reading the morning newspaper. She began to fill in the crossword puzzle. The one today was quite complicated. It was taking much longer than usual. "I suppose it doesn't matter," Madge murmured to herself. "I'm not going anywhere."

The door opened. Nurse Phillips entered the ward with a cup of tea. Madge put her pen and newspaper down and greeted Nurse Phillips with a warm smile. Nurse Phillips handed the cup to Madge.

"My, we're looking smart this morning. I love that shade of pink."

"Yes, Mar.. Someone bought it for me for Christmas. It's pretty isn't it?" Madge answered.

Nurse Phillips pulled up the chair by the bedside.

"I've got some good news for you. Doctor Tinsley is very pleased with your progress. He wants you to go on a home visit with the Occupational Therapist this afternoon to see how you can cope at home."

On hearing this, Madge became a little flustered.

"I can't do that. I've left my home and I'm staying with my sister."

"Yes we know. We're taking you to your sister's home later today to see how you get on. We'll ask your sister to take a back seat because we want to see how you manage. You'll be asked to make a cup of tea and put on toast and things like that."

Madge's face lit up with sheer delight.

"That's wonderful. At last I'll be able to see Andy," she exclaimed joyously.

A slight frown crossed Nurse Phillip's face.

"I'm sorry Andy isn't there."

Madge looked at her in bewilderment.

"Isn't there, what do you mean he isn't there? Where is he? What's happened to him?" Her voice rose shrilly. Her brow furrowed in deep concern. She became more and more agitated with every word.

Nurse Phillips looked surprised.

"I thought you knew. Andy's away on holiday."

"How can he be away on holiday, he's staying at my sister Mary's home."

"He's gone on a short holiday with your husband to Nice."

Madge interrupted her, "Nice? France? Mark?"

"Yes, your sister told me they've gone to the Carnival for a couple of days."

At this, Madge exploded.

"Mary. But I told her. She's no sister of mine. I told...Why hasn't anyone consulted me?" Madge's face flushed with distress. By now, she was getting very angry.

"At the time it was arranged you were really too poorly to be consulted." Nurse Phillips replied.

Madge was speechless. What could she do laid in this hospital bed? Madge fell back limply onto the pillow. This was too much to handle.

Nurse Phillips took hold of Madge's hand and spent the next half hour calming her down. Eventually, she was sufficiently composed for Nurse Phillips to leave her with her newspaper in her hand.

Madge was too anxious to read and kept worrying about Andy. The worry kept going round and round in her mind as if it had taken root there. It was like an old fashioned record on a turntable. Try as she could there was no way she could dislodge it.

All she could think about was why had Mark changed so much these last two years when previously he had been such a loving Dad.

She knew deep in her heart Mark was dangerous. Yes, he hadn't hurt Andy yet but if he were provoked what would he do? She felt he was capable of anything.

.

CHAPTER TWENTY ONE

Arriving in Los Angeles, California, they made their way to their friend, Roger. They knew he would believe them and would be able to help them.

Getting out of bed early was not one of Andy's strong points. He leisurely opened his eyes. The room was almost pitch-black. For a moment, he wondered where he was. He remembered he was in Nice in France.

Excitedly, he jumped out of bed; the huge duvet trailing with him. With some difficulty he went to the windows. He opened the large green shutters which were excluding the light. He started back, amazed, as he was met with a blaze of sunshine which poured gloriously into his bedroom.

He glanced at the empty bed next to him and wondered where his Dad was. He noticed the sound of running water in the bathroom which obviously gave him a good clue.

He looked out of the window and was mesmerised by the sight of a cavalcade of lorries. They were all decorated with flowers.

Every one was nose to tail. Each display was different. On every single lorry float he saw people decorated with flowers.

He heard the sound of a band in the distance. He loved the sound of marches played by a brass band.

"Dad, Dad," he shouted enthusiastically, "what's going on?"

His Dad emerged smiling from the bathroom, his shaver still in his hand.

He patiently explained about the Carnival in Nice. It was in February or March each year. This year, they were having an extra Carnival in August as an experiment.

"Can we go out and look properly?" Andy asked.

"Yes," replied his Dad. "We have to have a quick Continental breakfast before we go."

"Continental breakfast?" enquired Andy.

"Yes," his Dad explained. "It's a croissant which is bread which is shaped in a crescent. We have jam and coffee with it."

Quickly, Andy dressed. They went down into the hotel dining room.

The two ladies, the ones who had arrived late in the trolley car at the plane, were seated at a nearby table. They waved Mark and Andy across.

Mark and the ladies passed some pleasantries. The ladies were delighted to find fellow English speaking people. They did not to want to let Mark go.

They insisted Mark and Andy sit at their table. Andy was getting increasingly frustrated because they talked non-stop.

Andy hurriedly ate his breakfast but to no avail. His Dad took things at a more leisurely pace. He appeared to enjoy the company of these two elderly English ladies.

They showed him a brochure they obtained, all about Nice. They pointed out the museums, libraries, the university, the international art school.

They told him they were going to hear Nice opera that night.

"It would be lovely if you could join us," said the younger woman.

"They're showing Die Fledermaus by Johann Strauss tonight. I love Die Fledermaus," said the older lady. Turning to Andy she said, "Die Fledermaus means the bat."

"Yes, I know your son will love the party scene," added her sister. "It's all such fun and wonderful music."

At long last breakfast was over. Andy let out an inaudible sigh of relief.

Andy and Mark escaped into the fresh air amongst the mass of people and floats.

Andy was utterly bewildered by the sight of so many flowers. Each lorry had a different pageant or display beautifully made out of flowers.

Everywhere were flowers. Flowers were strewn on the road; flowers were strewn on the pavements. People were holding and throwing flowers.

The air was filled with the wonderful heady scent of the flowers.

One of the loveliest of fragrances was the yellow mimosa which is prevalent in this part of France.

The people on the floats were dressed in a wide array of costumes.

Suddenly, the procession set off with the sound from the band permeating the air. Andy and his Dad walked alongside for a while.

As Andy looked round, he noticed the two ladies. They were on the edge of the carriageway. They were walking on the opposite side of the road. They waved enthusiastically to Andy and Mark as if they were old long-lost friends.

Andy gave a reasonable imitation of a hearty wave back. They seemed absolutely enthralled with all they saw.

It was easy to spot them as they were dressed in very colourful clothes. They were a mixture of red, yellow and blue. In any other surrounding they would look garish. Here they looked right. They came prepared for the occasion.

Their outfit gave Andy an idea.

"I'm running back to the hotel, Dad."

Before Mark could stop him, Andy was off. He elbowed his way through the multitude. He weaved across the dual carriageway between the floats.

He pushed his way through the hordes of people on the other pavement. Finally, he reached the hotel.

He waited impatiently for the lift. Once inside the lift, it seemed to take for ever.

He emerged from the lift and ran down the corridor to his bedroom.

He changed into Chinese style pyjamas his Dad had bought him from one of his trips. They were a bright shiny red.

The tunic had little red and gold woven buttons down the front. The same buttons were on both cuffs. Over the front of the pyjama top was plenty of red and gold braid.

The trousers were of the same bright shiny red but were plain. He had a little Chinese cap to match. He looked at himself in the mirror and felt very smart.

This time, he did not wait for the lift. He energetically ran down the stairs – all five flights. He skipped through the entrance hall of the hotel. He went through the swing doors. He gave a beaming smile to the startled doorman.

Once outside, in the lovely warm sunshine, he looked for his Dad. He was nowhere to be seen. For a moment he panicked, and then he thought; "now I can do what I want!"

He scrambled onto the back of one of the floats where there were some other children. He smiled at them. They smiled back.

They started speaking to him. At first they gabbled away at him. Once they realised he did not understand them, they spoke more slowly.

Other than 'Bon jour' he did not understand a word. He determined he would make more effort in his French lessons next term.

They made several attempts to talk with Andy, without success. After a while, they gave up and chatted amongst themselves.

Andy did not mind for there was too much going on for him to be lonely.   "Now this was more like it......being part of the pageant," he thought.

As they travelled along the Promenade des Anglais he saw his Dad and waved.

His Dad signalled frantically for him to descend from the float. Andy pretended he did not understand.

Mark tried to get to him. He pushed his way through the throng but the crowd was too dense. Waves of people seemed to envelop him. By the time Mark was able to get to the road, the float had gone.

It was only a glimpse but Andy was sure he saw the two men coming towards him. If he had been able to hear them he would have been very worried.

One man turned to the other.

"This is our chance to grab the boy. His Dad can't get to him."

"Yes, you go one side of his float and I will go the other."

"We will have to make some excuse about his Dad sending us or he won't get down. If he struggles there would be ructions. We don't want a load of people calling the Police."

They hurried across toward Andy. They pushed hard against the throng of people. They tried to weave one way and then the other. Like his Dad, they were thwarted by the crowd.

The float Andy was on travelled east along the Promenade des Anglais and crossed over the River Paillon. They went past the harbour with its mixture of commercial vessels, fishing craft and pleasure boats and went inland into the old town.

The medieval old town is at the base of a granite hill which is called Le Chateau. The Castle which used to be on top, after which it was named, had been destroyed some four hundred years earlier.

They travelled down some narrow winding streets. They were very constricted. It seemed as if you could lean out of a window at one side of the road and touch the hand of someone in a house opposite.

The lorry came to an abrupt halt. The other children jumped off and ran down the street.

Before Andy realised what was happening, the lorry started its journey again, swiftly picking up speed. It went down some more streets with old fashioned buildings on either side. It came to an abrupt halt down a quiet back alley.

The engine of the vehicle ran for a minute or two before being switched off. Andy heard the bang of both doors of the lorry. He overheard the two men who descended from the cab of the lorry chatting. As it was all in French, he had no idea what they were saying.

"Why, oh why didn't I work harder at French at school?" he thought.

They casually threw bags over their shoulders and walked away. He wondered whether to call out. He was too petrified to do so. Silence descended.

Andy felt his heart thumping. He looked round. There was no-one to be seen. What did he do now? If he left the lorry, how would he find his way back? If he stayed with the lorry, how long would it before they came back. What would they say when they found him.

He contemplated the options open to him and realised he had a worrying dilemma.

Andy was beginning to feel sleepy. His eyes were heavy. He had difficulty keeping them open. Perhaps it was jet lag catching up with him.

He lay down on the floor of the lorry and was soon fast asleep amongst the flowers.

CHAPTER TWENTY TWO

Pete and Harry looked surreptitiously around before they approached Roger's flat. They hoped against hope he were in.

Madge's face crinkled in concern as she thought about what Nurse Phillips told her.

She was ready to tear a strip or two off Auntie Mary when she arrived at her home. How could she let Mark take Andy?

This was too much to bear. She trusted her sister. Now she had let her down. Who else could she trust?

She realised she would have to be careful with Auntie Mary as she needed her with her plan to alienate Andy from his Father. She ran through her plan again in her mind and smiled to herself as she thought how clever she was.

It wasn't going to be easy being pleasant with Auntie Mary but she could not fall out with her now as her help was vital to the success of her scheme.

She picked up a magazine and glanced at it but she couldn't concentrate.

She was beginning to get a little impatient as she waited for the Orderlies to take her on her home visit. She kept glancing at her watch.

Meanwhile, Joe and Mike travelled along the country lanes to the Manchester hospital where Madge was. It was quite a feat negotiating all the country roads in a large ambulance. They were pleased when they arrived in the City area with its wider roads.

"You said she can be moved in a wheelchair," said Joe "so why are we in this huge bus of an ambulance?"

"Beggars can't be chooses and that was all I managed to steal." replied Mike.

They pulled up outside the hospital. Mike parked up a little bit away from the entrance. Joe put on a white overall. He unloaded the wheelchair and entered the hospital. He looked round furtively. He looked at Mike's written instructions. He thought "It's a good thing Mike phoned the night before and found out where Madge is."

He tried to be nonchalant as he pushed the wheelchair along the corridors. He arrived at Madge's room.

She was pleased to hear a hesitant knock at her door. It opened. A tall man in a white overall came in. A white mask covered the lower part of his face so she could not see him properly.

"He must be the one taking me for my home trial," thought Madge.

He pushed the wheelchair into the brightly lit room. He pushed it alongside her bed. He lifted her roughly from her bed into the wheel chair. She winced in pain. She was not going to say anything which might stop her home visit. However, she was surprised a hospital orderly was so insensitive. "It must be because they are doing it all day." She thought.

He covered her legs with a blanket from her bed. Whilst she had his back to him, he pushed her pillows 'human shape' down the bed.

He mumbled something about an ambulance. He quickly pushed her along the hospital corridors. In fact, he was almost running with her down the corridors. He seemed to be in an unseemly haste.

Outside a shorter, rather rough looking man was standing by an ambulance. He, too, wore a white coat and a white face mask.

Joe knocked at the driver's window.

"Mike come and help me get her in."

"OK Joe," replied Mike.

Mike opened his door. He jumped out and ran round to the back of the ambulance. He flung open the doors at the rear. He assisted Joe lift Madge into the back.

They lifted the wheel chair together. They clamped it into place with Madge still sitting in it. She was marooned in the middle of the large ambulance.

The two men went round to the front, got in and drove off rapidly. The two men were talking between themselves. Madge was unable to hear what they said as there was an internal window between her section of the ambulance and the front.

The windows of the ambulance were darkened. Although it was a sunny day, Madge could not see very well out of them.

It was lovely to be out of the hospital and see life again. It seemed such a long time since she was on the outside.

They sped through the town and into the countryside. Madge felt sick as they speedily negotiated country roads with their multitude of turns.

She recognised when they arrived in the village where Auntie Mary lived. She was baffled when they did not slow down. Madge was even more staggered when they passed the turning to her sister's home. She called out to the ambulance men.

"We've just passed the way to my sister's avenue. Where are we going?"

The one who had opened the ambulance doors answered her rather gruffly.

"That's not for you to know. Be quiet and you won't get hurt."

.

CHAPTER TWENTY THREE

"The first thing we've to do," said Roger, "is find a first class lawyer so he can look at all the papers. I know just the man. I'll ring him straight away."

Sammy climbed down from the ledge to the waiting children. They looked expectantly at him. His gloomy expression told them all. He was at quite a loss as to how to put it. In the end, there was no wrapping it up.

"I can't open the lid," he said bluntly.

"Can't open the lid," chorused Maisie and Danny together.

A look of alarm spread across their faces. Danny believed Sammy could do anything.

Although the brothers sparred frequently and Danny was usually the underdog, he loved and respected his brother fiercely.

When they first started secondary school there was a big problem. Some of the older boys came up and challenged them. They found it funny Sammy and Danny were identical twins. They found it funny they had red hair. They found it funny they had loads of freckles. Everything they found funny about them.

They had a real go at Danny because he was slightly shorter than Sammy. They saw Danny as a bookworm, a swot.

They reckoned without Sammy's fierce loyalty and courage. As they taunted Danny, Sammy intervened and stood up for Danny. A fight broke out. Sammy proved to be an excellent fighter. They backed off. Trouble at school was rare after that. Yes, in his heart of hearts, Danny believed Sammy could do anything.

"I'll go up and try again," said Danny with a boldness he did not feel. Climbing onto the top ledge, he pushed with all his might but to no avail.

It was clear someone had put the catch back in place.

His face was grim when he reached the other two.

"What are we going to do?" asked Maisie with quite a whine in her voice. She was very alarmed at this turn of events. She had known Sammy and Danny a long time. She knew they were resourceful. She was not convinced they could get them out of this predicament.

"We can sit here until we die or we can have a Council meeting," said Sammy taking charge.

"We'll go and sit on the floor and see if we can come up with an idea," he continued.

"But we could be here forever," said Maisie fearfully.

"Stop that," said Sammy bossily. "Sit there and think and think hard."

Maisie did not know whether to be more scared of never escaping from the tunnel or of Bossy Boots.

She sat down very promptly. The floor was cold and uninviting. She was glad she had the forethought to put her smart blue raincoat on. She remembered from the last time they were underground, it may be a sunny day in the garden but it did not mean it was warm in the tunnel.

Sammy was also very scared but he did not want to show it. He particularly did not want a girl to know he was scared.

"What if we never got out?" he thought. "We will become white skeletons like the ones in the Biology class." He suppressed a worried sigh.

They sat and discussed the matter fully. It was soon apparent their options were very limited.

They could wait and see if someone released the catch. Perhaps, Andy might return early and come and look. They decided it was unlikely Andy would return early.

Anyone else who came to release the catch was likely to come down into the tunnel and find them and that might spell trouble.

They could knock loudly on the lid but Andy was away and Auntie Mary never visited that part of the garden.

The only people who may visit would be the ones who knew about the tunnel. If they were to come it would be a big problem.

They could go down the left tunnel. They were concerned about what Andy described to them when he looked out. They were particularly concerned about the two vicious-looking men he saw.

If they went that way there was a serious possibility they may have difficulty in getting to safety. If they were caught who knows what would happen. The idea did not bear thinking about.

They were in a quandary.

Ponderously and emphatically Danny took centre stage. He spoke slowly and deliberately.

"It's been a huge puzzlement to me." His steady voice failed to betray the enormity of his idea.

"A puzzlement, why people dig out a room a long way down the second tunnel?" he paused for effect. "Why didn't they build it alongside the end of the left tunnel?"

Seeing their surprised look, he continued.

"Why did they make the door close so quickly behind them when they would see and hear if anyone came down the tunnel? Another question I ask myself is - how would they get all their machines out?"

He saw the other two were looking at him with rapt attention. Their teachers at school would have been delighted to see this level of concentration.

"I think," again he paused for effect, "I think there's another way out of that room!"

You could have heard a pin drop.

"Well, what are we waiting for?" said Sammy, once again taking charge.

With some haste, the three of them set off down the tunnel.

Suddenly, Maisie let out the most blood-curdling scream you could imagine. She froze to the spot absolutely scared stiff.

The two boys turned round and looked at her with amazement.

She stood there very still, her eyes and mouth wide open.

She continued to scream at the top of her voice. It was loud and penetrating and hurt the ear drums.

At first, they could not get any sense out of her. Eventually, she managed to stutter, "a, a ,a rat ran over my foot." By now the screams turned to loud sobs of fear.

The two boys fell about laughing.

"What's a rat or two between friends," they jokingly said.

Through her tears, Maisie glared at them.

"Stop you two, you're being unkind."

They were enjoying the joke too much to cease their merriment.

"Wait till we get back to school and tell them Maisie was frightened of a rat," said Sammy flippantly.

At that moment, another rat brushed against Sammy. It was his turn to be shocked. He tried not to show he was frightened.

"We'd better hurry or we'll be here all night."

Once again, the three of them walked along the cut-out way, a little more warily than before, a little more apprehensively than before. Inside all of them, hearts were beating faster than normal.

As they reached the junction of the two tunnels, the torch Sammy was carrying dimmed.

"That's all we need," he thought, "for the torch to extinguish."

By the time they reached the wall it was increasingly difficult to see.

Sammy could have kicked himself for not bringing an extra battery. He was taught always to be prepared. He was not prepared for this eventuality.

At the wall, Danny hurriedly knelt on the floor. He gingerly felt round until he felt the lever. He knew the right direction to pull it this time and easily pulled the lever.

The children were thrilled to hear a grating noise as the door swung slowly open.

The three of them hovered at the entrance to the doorway. They knew once they stepped over the threshold they were committed.

They continued to pause at the open door. They glanced at each other; as one man they rushed into the cave. The door shut quickly behind them.

.

CHAPTER TWENTY FOUR

"The two men set off to the Lawyer's. Their heart was in their mouth from fear of being spotted."

Nurse Phillips bounced into Madge's room. What a wonderful and enjoyable encounter with Doctor Tinsley. She could not believe it were true. Her heart was still pounding.

She was standing by the coffee machine during her morning break. Doctor Tinsley walked over to her. Her heart fluttered quite a bit as he drew near.

"Anne," yes he called her Anne, "I need to discuss some things with you. I wondered if you will be free this evening."

"This evening," what did he mean? She finished early today. Perhaps he wanted her to come back for the evening shift.

"Yes, I can come back to the hospital this evening."

"No, would you come out for a meal with me?"

"Ooooh, Doctor," she gasped . She was stunned, excited, all the emotions in the world rolled into one: THE Doctor Tinsley inviting her out.

As she left him, she was walking on air. Nothing in the world could be wrong now they were going out to dinner.

"Madge," she enthused, "I've good news. The men will be here in about half an hour to take you home. I've come to help get you ready."

When there was no response from Madge. Nurse Phillips walked over to the bed.

"Madge, are you alright?" Nurse Phillips voice turned to deep concern. She pulled the bedclothes back. No Madge, only pillows!

Bewildered, Nurse Phillips looked round the room, even under the bed. She went out and searched the bathrooms. Puzzled, she went up to reception. She asked if anyone had seen Madge Appleyard. No-one had.

Breathlessly, she went to see Doctor Tinsley. He looked astounded, particularly when she explained about the pillows.

"Come with me," he said.

It was quite a walk through the hospital campus hospital to Security. In normal circumstances Nurse Phillips would be delighted to be spending so much time with Doctor Tinsley.

Doctor Tinsley explained what had happened to the man at Security. He explained Madge was last seen at eight thirty that morning. Nurse Phillips looked on with deep concern.

The security man was very helpful.

PESHA

"Come through to the viewing area."

He went over to a television screen. He pushed some buttons. A video played. There was quite a bit of movement on it as various people walked about the hospital.

Suddenly, Nurse Phillips called out, "stop, can you rewind that bit."

Carefully, the security man rewound the video. He put the next couple of minutes on loop so it kept replaying.

"Can you enlarge it?" asked Doctor Tinsley.

There was no mistaking it was Madge being pushed in a wheel chair.

"That's a puzzle," said Nurse Phillips, "the ambulance men said they weren't coming until eleven o'clock."

"At least, it's a mystery solved," replied Doctor Tinsley.

"Yes, I will get on to them straightaway. Why would they put pillows down her bed?" Why has he a mask on?" replied Nurse Phillips.

"Maybe the pillow landed that way as they assisted her out of bed and as to the mask, I agree that's highly unusual," the Doctor replied.

Nurse Phillips went round to the ambulance station. She thought it better to go in person than telephone. She felt something was very wrong.

They were equally puzzled. No one had been sent from their end to collect Madge.

By now, Nurse Phillips was getting very worried. She returned to see Doctor Tinsley. This was not the way she

164

anticipated spending time with him.

After a brief discussion, Doctor Tinsley rang Management.

To Nurse Phillips, it seemed like hours before the Police arrived. In reality it was only fifteen minutes. They questioned and took a statement from her.

Nurse Phillips had the forethought to look in Madge's locker where she found the Court papers and the torn up envelope and letter. She handed them to the Police.

They interviewed Security and took the video. Later in the day they brought in Forensic.

CHAPTER TWENTY FIVE

Mr. Peterson looked every bit a trial lawyer. His portly figure told something about his life style. He listened carefully to Pete and Harry and advised them.

Norma spent all day at the County Court on one of her many cases. Her caseload, as she called it.

She loved her job because it was very varied. Some days, she was in Court giving evidence. Other days, she was visiting people in their homes. She had plenty of paperwork to do when she returned to the office each evening. Sometimes, her work was very frustrating. Some days, nothing seemed to go right.

Today, she had not expected to be at Court very long. She thought it was a straightforward case. Her recommendation to the Court was effortless to write. Unexpectedly, it turned out to be a very long hard day at Court.

The Barrister for the Father (or Counsel, as they called themselves,) asked her endless questions. In fact, he questioned, cross-examined her, for an hour and a half. Norma was surprised the Judge let him go on so long.

In Norma's mind, her report was straightforward. The Mother moved some two hundred and fifty miles away with their daughter, Sarah, who was aged ten. The Father, sadly, had a condition which prevented him travelling. The Father wanted his daughter to come up and see him every fortnight.

Norma was passionate Fathers saw their children. She considered it unreasonable a little girl travelled a round trip of some five hundred mile every fortnight

Norma thought their daughter, Sarah, should come up for a few days each holiday, including half-terms, and for a fortnight during the summer holiday.

To be fair to the Father, it was not his choice the Mother moved such a long way a way. The Court appreciated the Mother needed to relocate in order to pursue her career path.

When the couple lived in the same town contact with their daughter was easy to arrange and worked very well. Sarah saw her Father twice a week. She regularly stayed over at weekends. He had her for long periods during the holidays.

It was obvious to Norma, Sarah loved her Dad; she loved both her parents very much. She was a sensible, intelligent young lady who worked hard at school and was doing very well.

She had taken the break up of her parent's marriage well. Underneath, there were fears she was unable to express even to Norma. What Sarah wanted was her parents live together in the same house.

Sarah was unhappy living faraway from her Dad. She understood her Mum was not doing it deliberately to get away from her Dad: it was the only place in the country she could obtain employment in her chosen field.

Counsel for the Father was persistent and penetrating in his cross-examination. In some ways, Norma felt he was cheeky in some of the questions he asked.

He seemed to think if the Father paid the train fare there was no reason why Sarah could not come.

He paid no regard to the life the Mother wanted to lead. The Court regarded the Mother as the Primary Carer. She saw to Sarah's needs every day.

Because the Father could not travel, she had to bring her daughter up to the North every fortnight. The result was a very tired Sarah when they returned home. Getting Sarah up for school the next morning was nightmare. It was essential nothing interfered with the quality of her studying. This was not a positive outcome.

No, Norma was very clear in her recommendation in this case.

The Judge listened very carefully to Norma and her objections to fortnightly contact.

The parents gave evidence next. It was an Application by the Father for extended contact so he gave his evidence first.

A picture emerged of a devoted father who helped greatly in the upbringing of his daughter. He was a lecturer at the College and was able to spend a great deal of time with his daughter in the long holiday periods.

Unfortunately, he had a severe accident in the College. A machine, he was using, completely severed his arm. This, in itself, would not have stopped him travelling. It was all the trauma which had a deep effect on his inmost being. He did not want to be involved in any machines whether they were in a workshop or whether they travelled on a road or rail.

While he was off recuperating from College, he spent a lot more time with Sarah. This gave his wife more time to develop her career. An extra strong bond grew between Sarah and him.

His world fell apart one day when his wife announced she was leaving him. The accident wrecked their marriage. The Mother moved to a new home fairly close to the matrimonial home. She took Sarah with her. Happily there was frequent contact.

He thought his wife leaving him was the worst thing that could happen to him. He loved her dearly. He could not understand why she was leaving him. She made it clear there was no-one else in her life.

But it got worse. One day his wife announced she was moving to the South of England. She explained, she put in multiple job applications. This was the only one which gave her career the boost it needed.

Now, he was a broken man. In one fell swoop he was losing seeing his wife and his daughter. Thus, he made the Application to the Court to see his daughter regularly.

The Father was asked a number of questions by the upstart Barrister. Then, it was the turn of his wife to give evidence.

She gave her evidence clearly and precisely. She found it too difficult to cope with her husband after his accident. He had become very precise and meticulous. He couldn't bear any untidiness in the home. He would shout at Sarah if she failed to put away the book she was reading.

She moved out of their home into rented accommodation. She tried to advance herself. She realised she had to move. She uprooted to the South of England and took out a mortgage on a terraced house. She found a school for Sarah nearby.

The Father's Barrister manfully cross-examined the Mother. He was unable to move her from her viewpoint. She did not think Sarah should be up and down the country like a yo-yo.

The Barristers delivered their closing speeches. They emphasised the good points in their clients' favour.

The Judge gave his judgment carefully and meticulously. He was impressed by both parents. He felt Norma's recommendation was the more realistic way forward and in the best interest of Sarah.

Norma knew the Judge did not rubber stamp her view. He was certainly encouraged by the Higher Courts such as the Court of Appeal to give very clear reasons if he did not wish to follow her recommendation.

Norma returned to headquarters, grabbed a quick coffee and retired to the tranquillity of her own office.

She made a detailed report of the day. She made a note to warn others of the upstart Barrister. He was clearly a new boy. Although, she had to admit, rather wryly, he asked some very insightful questions.

She wished it was as easy to write her recommendations in other cases. The Appleyard case, for instance, there was something that did not quite add up. Norma had a niggle in her mind for some time and she was unable to put her finger on it.

Norma looked down at the papers on her desk.

Another CAFCASS officer put her head round Norma's door.

"Hi Norma, "you're working late," said Julie Jarvis.

"Yes." Norma recounted details of her difficult day.

"Can I run something by you?" asked Norma.

"Of course, you can. That's what we're here for - to help each other."

Julie was a real asset. She joined the Service a couple of years earlier. Nothing seemed to be too much trouble for her.

Norma outlined the details of the background and recent history of the Appleyard case.

"Does something strike you as strange?" Norma asked.

Julie paused before answering.

"I find it strange the Father seemed to be an excellent Father until about two years ago. Usually, where there's violence, there's a continual history of violence."

Norma nodded in agreement.

"Did anything happen about two years ago? Was there a change in this family's life?" Julie asked.

"Yes, the Father changed his job."

Even as she said it, the niggle was illuminated. She knew the investigation she must make.

CHAPTER TWENTY SIX

What was vital was they obtained some supportive documents which corroborated their story. They asked how they could acquire them.

Andy woke with a start. The float was on the move again. He looked at his watch. It was four in the afternoon. He must have slept for several hours. He grimaced slightly as he wondered what his Dad would say.

He knew he was going to be in big trouble. He hated it when his Dad got angry. Mind you, even Andy realised it was justified on this occasion.

Thoughts of home came flooding back to Andy. He longed to be back with his Mum and Dad living together. Why do grown ups fall out?

He was puzzled why his Dad had become so grumpy. They used to have a wonderful time together.

His Dad took him swimming. They larked around in the water together: throwing a ball at each other.

They picked up a pizza and chips on the way home. Andy loved his chips. He thought if there were no other food in the world, he would have to have his chips. He had to admit ice cream came a very close second. He licked his lips as he saw in his mind's eye the Knickerbockers Glory he had the other day.

His Dad took him each week to football. Andy loved to dress up in his town's colours which were predominantly black and white, except when they played away, when they were turquoise.

He played for his town's junior football team and was very proud of this. Sometimes, the team played matches at home, sometimes, they played away.

His Dad made a website for his team which carried the timetable of matches. There were also plenty of photographs of team members on it.

People from all round the world contacted them. Many of the team's relatives in other towns and countries expressed appreciation at being able to see the photographs on the Internet.

He loved it when his Mum came to matches. In the winter months, she dressed in warm clothes and heavy waterproof boots: a thick, warm, black and white scarf wrapped round her neck. She stood on the edge of the field cheering them all on, oft times to victory.

It was wonderful when his Mum and Dad came there together. It made him feel very special.

As he thought of his Mum and Dad, Andy felt home sick. He tried to push down his deep worry about his Mum. Would she live? Would she die? What would become of him? Why would no-one let him see her? Tears trickled down his face. He brushed them away; after all he was now the man of the house.

He tried to get up from the floor of the lorry to see where they were. As he did so, the lorry turned round a corner rather sharply. He fell down again. He slithered to one side of the lorry. He glanced over the edge. He was relieved to see the sea.

He wondered how he was going to get off the lorry. He realised he only had a few minutes to think before they might go down side streets again. Then what would become of him!

With some trepidation, he knew what he must do. Holding firmly to the side of the lorry, he waited his chance. When the lorry turned the next corner, Andy closed his eyes and jumped.

He seemed to bounce as he rolled into the gutter. Very gingerly, he wiggled his toes and his fingers. Nothing seemed to be broken. He stood up and winced. A sharp pain shot through his knee. His left arm was very, very painful. He was surprised no-one came and helped him but in some ways he was thankful about that. The last thing he wanted was a fuss.

Bit by bit he hobbled along the Promenade des Anglais until their hotel came into view.

The last hundred yards seemed for ever. He hurt all over. He was worried what his Dad would say. His Dad would certainly tear a strip off him these days. He thought ruefully.

How does one walk nonchalantly or rather hobble through one of the best hotels in Nice in a Chinese costume covered in dirt?

Andy felt every eye was on him as he crossed the large entrance hall of the hotel until he reached the lift.

Normally, he was entranced to hear all the people chattering away in different languages. Some were French, some were German, some were Italian and some were unrecognisable. This time, he was glad there was no-one else in the lift with him.

Limping along the corridor, he arrived at his room. He inserted the key into the lock and quietly let himself in.

Sitting on a blue swivel chair, his body silhouetted against the window, was his Dad. He appeared to be speaking to someone but Andy could not see anyone else in the room. Andy realised his Dad was talking on the telephone.

His Father was very agitated. He talked very rapidly. Long silences as his Dad listened to what was being said. From time to time the silences were punctured by, "oh no," and, "it can't be true."

At one point in the conversation Andy heard his Dad say "the Police."

"Oh dear," thought Andy, "I didn't mean things to turn out like this and have the Police involved."

Andy was gearing up his courage to tell his Dad he was there, when he heard him say, "kidnapped." Things were going from bad to worst thought Andy. He presumed it was about him missing all day.

Andy knew he was in big, big trouble if his Father thought he had been kidnapped and the Police had been called in. He realised how worried his Dad must be.

He was about to open his mouth and say he was there when he heard his Dad say, "Madge kidnapped."

"Dad, Dad," Andy called out, "what's happened to Mum?"

Mark spun round in his chair. Tears welled up in his eyes. He did not know how to react. Pleased his son was home. Cross because he had caused him so much anxiety. Cry because of the news he had heard about his wife being kidnapped. He still loved her dearly and could not understand why she had left him.

When his telephone call was finished, Mark looked at Andy very carefully. He saw the dirty smudges on his face where he had been crying. Mark put his arm around Andy and gently explained what had happened to his Mum.

Andy began to cry.

"Why've they taken my Mum? She's the best Mum in the world."

"Nobody knows," said Mark. He tried to have a puzzled look on his face as he told Andy part of the truth.

"We ought to be getting home to England as soon as possible," he continued.

Mark was so engrossed in hearing about Madge, he momentarily forgot about Andy's disappearance.

As it all came back to Mark, he looked at Andy with a mixture of sadness and anger.

"Where've you been all day? I've been worried sick about you."

Andy recounted the events of the day. As he did so, he snuggled up to his Dad and gave him a big hug. Andy certainly knew how to get round his Dad.

As Andy stood up, Mark realised Andy had suffered injuries in his leap from the lorry. He rang down to the reception and asked where the local Doctor was. The reception was very helpful. They explained they had a resident Doctor who would be up in a few minutes.

The Doctor was pleased to practise his English and listened intently as Andy told of all his adventures since joining the float. He cleaned up Andy's wounds. He put bandages on his knee and on his arm.

Andy was looking very much like the walking wounded.

After the Doctor left, Mark packed their bags. No Nice opera with the two English ladies that night.

Andy hobbled to the lift. After paying the hotel, they caught a taxi and went to the airport.

The wait at the airport was not as long as their outward journey. Andy and his Dad spent the time looking in the French boutiques which surrounded the waiting area. Mark bought some gifts to take home. He also bought some Grasse perfume for Madge.

As he purchased the perfume, he wondered when he would see Madge again. To say he was worried was an understatement.

It was a slow walk across the tarmacadam: an even slower walk up the gangway. They settled in their seats. How Andy's knee and arm throbbed. He did not know where to put them to be comfortable.

The engines revved up, the plane taxied down the runway and now they were airborne.

Andy was pleased to get a window seat again. He loved it when they were high up. It looked as if you could walk on the clouds.

As Andy looked out of the window, before they set off, he was dumbfounded to see the two men he had seen on emerging from the tunnel. He knew, without doubt, they were being followed.

.

CHAPTER TWENTY SEVEN

"I know a man who can withdraw the papers for you but he comes at a price," said the portly Lawyer. "We've no option," replied Pete.

Maisie and the twins knew there was no going back once they entered the cave.

Apprehensively, they stood in front of the closed door and looked round the cave. They were surprised to find the room lit up with bright fluorescent lights.

Everything was as they saw it before, but much clearer. The various shaped chemical bottles, the scales and other apparatus.

This time they could see the gyro machines much better. They gave off a glow in the bright light. They appeared to be high precision machinery.

Maisie was the first to move. She walked across to one of the benches to look more closely at the machines. With their bubble type heads, they looked more like an imitation of an Extra Terrestrial Being.

She carefully examined one of the machines. She looked into the container under the gyroscope which was firmly slotted into place and saw it was empty.

"I wonder what it's for?" she said half aloud and half to herself.

The twins joined her. They went from bench to bench absolutely fascinated by what they saw.

Suddenly a slight rustle was heard.

Maisie jumped.

"What was that?" she asked.

Visions of rats leaped around in her mind. There was no further sound so she thought she made a mistake.

When another rustle occurred, there was no mistake about that. Sammy and Danny blanched: their eyes showed fear. Hip to hip, they walked slowly towards the corner of the cave. It seemed much darker there than the rest of the room.

Again, they heard the rustle sound and an almost imperceptible moan. By now, their knees were shaking.

Although Danny was shyer than Sammy, there were times he showed an amazing boldness. This was one such occasion.

He left the side of Sammy. He made two or three strides until he came to an abrupt halt.

In the corner was a lady in her pink nightdress. She was curled up in a ball lying on the floor. She was tied up, bound and gagged. Her eyes were closed as if she were asleep.

Tentatively, Sammy and Maisie walked across the room and joined Danny. They stood there, open mouthed.

"What do we do now?" whispered Maisie.

"I think we should get out of here as quickly as possible," replied Sammy. In his fright his voice seemed to have dropped as deep as his Father's.

"If we get caught we'll land up like her," he continued.

"We can't leave her here all tied up," replied soft-hearted Maisie.

"Why not," said Sammy, "if we get caught we'll land up like her." He said again, as if he were on automatic pilot. Truth to tell he had never been so frightened in all his life.

"Sammy's right," said Danny in a low voice, "I think we should try and get out of here and get some help."

It was clear the lady was either drugged or knocked out in some way. Apart from the occasional moans, she did not seem to realise they were there.

"We'll have to find a way out," said Sammy, some of his composure returning.

Silently, the three of them walked round the room. They looked at the walls very intently. They hoped to find a crack in the wall which may indicate an exit. But none seemed to be there.

It was Danny who spoke next.

"I'm still convinced there's another way out of this cave. I think we should run our hands all along the floor near the wall and see if there's another lever."

The three of them got down on their hands and knees. They carefully ran their hands along the floor. It was a large cave so they spent quite a long time doing this.

Suddenly, Maisie called out, "I think I've found the lever."

The other two rushed to her side and got on the floor alongside Maisie.

The small lever was well up against the wall. It was almost diametrically opposite the entrance to the cave. They each took it in turn to pull it but it would not budge.

They looked at each other in despair.

"This must be the correct lever," said Danny, "I don't think we're trying to move it in the proper way."

As he spoke, he tried to turn the lever in circle. As he did so, a door opened in the wall in front of them. The form of a man filled the entrance. He was silhouetted against the daylight.

"Not so quick, my beauties," said the man as he grabbed Maisie and Danny. He carried them kicking and screaming outside. He started to take them down a long yard.

"Let my brother go," screamed Sammy. He kicked the man sharply on his ankle. The man let out a yell. He involuntarily let go of Danny but managed to hold on to Maisie. She wriggled, and screamed. She tried to kick the man but to no avail.

Danny and Sammy ran away. As they reached the far end of the long yard, they stopped.

"We can't leave Maisie with that man," they said in unison.

They ran back. They ran into the arms of another man who emerged from a nearby hut.

The two men tied the three children up. They put them back in the cave next to the lady. By this time, she had woken up and looked wide-eyed at what was going on. She knew better than to speak.

"What are we going to do with our prisoners?" asked the taller man. "The children, particularly, know too much if they've got into the cave."

"I don't know," replied the other. "We'll have to wait until the Boss gets back from France."

"I think we should kill them now. Replied the taller man" As he spoke he produced a long sharp knife.

.

CHAPTER TWENTY EIGHT

Very nervously Pete, Harry and the Lawyer went down town. Their eyes were everywhere looking out for the cops. They knew there would be a good reward on their heads.

Norma drew up outside Mark's home in Robina. Her old jalopy certainly gave good service. She wondered what she would do when she had to change cars.

Today, she decided not to bring the student with her for this interview. All interviews were sensitive and fraught with problems. But with all the extra trauma of Madge's hospitalisation and kidnapping, she felt this case needed extra delicacy in her handling of it.

Gathering together her papers, she alighted from the car. She walked up the garden path which was filled with all sorts of flowers.

Norma was surprised to see a mixture of vegetable plants with flowers in the front garden. She saw the Globe Artichoke with its huge thistle like flowers and their edible scales. Nearby were orangey-yellow courgette flowers amongst the tall elegant blue delphiniums. These, in turn, intermingled with the yellow French Marigolds. Amongst them was a mixture of multi-coloured pansies with their dark velvet faces.

On one side was a mass of rose bushes. Set between them were onion and garlic plants.

"I guess it's all part of the synergy of nature," she thought to herself.

She walked up to Mark's impressive black door somewhat nervously. She knocked firmly on the large brass knocker.

She hated these first few moments when she did not know what sort of reception she would get.

In this case, she need not have worried. Mark opened the door and warmly welcomed her in. The smell of freshly-made coffee permeated the air.

Mark showed her into a large comfortable lounge. Here, an old fashioned log fire blazed warmly. They had a super warm spell lately but today had turned cold. Norma was glad of the warmth of the fire.

The settee and the armchairs were arranged invitingly around the fire. On the walls were photographs of the family and some paintings.

"Can I get you a cup of coffee?" asked Mark.

Yes, thank you."

Whilst Mark went to make the coffee, Norma looked around at the room with interest.

Some of the photographs, on a ledge at her side, were near enough for her to take down. She chose one and looked at it more carefully.

It was a large colour photograph with a picture of the three of them, Madge, Mark and Andy. They were in their large back garden and looked very happy together.

The photo also displayed the gardening expertise of someone in the family which Norma noticed in the front garden.

All over the garden was a wide spread of flowers and vegetables. The multi-coloured sweet peas were particularly attractive against the varied colours of the antirrhinums. In the centre was a small, well cut lawn.

When she turned the photograph over, she saw the date was only a year earlier.

Norma thought to herself she did not often get into such cosy homes. "What," she wondered, "had gone wrong in the family relationships?"

Mark returned with the steaming coffee and a cake which Aunt Mary had given him.

Norma decided to keep to her usual method of addressing the parent by their first name.

"Mark, I'm Norma Brent, the CAFCASS Officer, please feel free to call me Norma."

"Do sit down, Norma," said Mark warmly.

Norma sat down in an arm chair alongside the fire place. Mark sat back in an arm chair opposite Norma.

His relaxed posture belying the anxiety he felt and the deep worry about Madge being kidnapped.

After sipping the coffee, Norma brought out her note book out of the black, leather briefcase she carried.

"I've to make notes of the interview. I use them to write my report for the Court. I want to run through some basic questions first. Later, on I want to see Andy alone."

Gradually, Norma felt Mark relax, as he answered her questions about himself. She moved on in her questioning and asked about Andy.

At times, his face became quite animated, as he discussed the things Andy and he did together.

He told her of the wonderful holiday they had in Nice, France. He was careful to omit any details of Andy's escapade with the lorry float. He was feeling rather guilty about that episode. He was worried it would count against him.

The relaxed and free conversation came to an abrupt halt when they started to discuss the relationship between him and Madge. Norma saw him visibly stiffen up.

He was prepared to admit their relationship was poor for the last two years. He could not understand what had gone wrong. He agreed he was more short-tempered since he started his new job. He denied hitting Madge. He suggested she misinterpreted a move he made to help her, when she was in a state of distress.

Mark's denial and the reference to his new job set off warning bells ringing in Norma's mind, "I really must investigate this further," she thought.

She skilfully probed further as to the nature of his work. Somewhat reluctantly, he explained, it was a secret chemical process. However hard she tried she could not get him to elaborate further.

With a little frustration, Norma changed the topic. She questioned Mark on his relationship with his son.

She was secretly deeply concerned at the news of the French holiday.

She felt more enquiries were needed before Mark had such a free amount of contact with his son. On the other hand, it was important Andy knew both his parents. This was particularly important with the bizarre circumstances of his Mother's disappearance.

"This might be the right moment for me to have a chat with Andy, is he ....." Norma asked.

"Yes," said Mark, interrupting her. "He's upstairs playing in his bedroom.

He has a computer up there and is quite a whiz kid on it. I've seen his school work improve tremendously since he started to do research on the Internet.

I took him back to Auntie Mary's after we returned from France. I went and collected him from her home this morning. I'll call him."

Mark went out of the room to the foot of the stairs. He called Andy down.

Andy came into the room with a slightly cocky air. This was his way of dealing with nervousness.

"Hello Andy," said Norma, "come and join us."

The next few minutes were an opportunity for Norma to see how Andy related to his Dad. She was pleased there was a real bond between them.

Norma was astute enough to notice a number of model planes at the far end of the room.

"Have you made those planes?" She asked.

A wide beam lit up Andy's face. Soon he was talking vivaciously about his model planes. Apparently, he spent most of his pocket money on buying kits and making them up. When they were assembled, he enjoyed painting them in the correct colours. He was very sorry his Mother had not allowed him to take his collection to Auntie Mary's home.

At the first opportunity, Mark discreetly went out of the room. He left them chatting like old friends.

Adroitly, Norma brought the conversation round to his Mum and Dad. She needed to know Andy's wishes and feelings about the whole situation so she could recount them to the Court.

At the mention of his Mum, Andy's face lit up.

"Have you found my Mum? Can I see her?

Norma explained the hospital was making all enquiries and the Police had set up a special unit to help find her.

"When they've found her will I be able to see her?" Andy asked.

"I'm sure we can arrange that."

At this, Andy relaxed as he thought of seeing his Mum soon. He opened up to her like a flower in spring. He told of how he loved his Mum and Dad very much. How he wanted them to live together like they used to do.

He admitted his Dad was a bit cross lately but he loved him just the same.

His eyes lit up as he told of the excitement of going to France. He knew he did not know Norma well enough to tell her of the tunnel or of his suspicions concerning the two men.

Norma pressed Andy a little more to try and find out where he would like to live.

"Who would you like to live with, your Mum or your Dad?"

Andy's eyes clouded. He lowered and shook his head.

"What does that mean?" asked Norma gently.

He pondered for a moment. He thought about his Mum and he was missing her so much. He thought about his Dad, he missed his Dad and all the things they did together.

He really wanted to live with them both but it seemed that was not going to happen. He wondered why grown ups fell out for a long time. When he fell out with a friend they soon made up.

What was he to say? Then he knew the answer. His Mum had Auntie Mary and his Dad had no-one.

He lifted his head. Norma saw a proud glint in his eye. She would have loved to have known what was going on in his head.

"With my Dad," he firmly answered.

Norma's heart sank when she heard Andy's reply. She knew the Courts took a lot of account of what a child of Andy's age would say.

Superficially, Mark was alright. However there were too many unanswered questions for her to feel Andy was really safe with his Dad long term.

CHAPTER TWENTY NINE

They entered a seedy looking building. They climbed narrow wooden steps which must have been a hundred years old. They furtively knocked at a flat door. A scrawny middle-aged man opened it. So this was Charlie: the best in the business.

Madge did not know whether to be pleased or deeply sad to find three children next to her in the cave. She was pleased to have some company but was very worried for them.

The three children were still shaking with fright. Their faces were deathly white. They were huddled up together in the corner.

The children looked at Madge in bewilderment. She looked at them in a similar manner. Each was wondering why the other was there.

It was Maisie who first spoke, "I want my Mummy."

As she spoke, tears flowed freely down her already grubby cheeks.

Madge tried to drag herself nearer and cuddle up to her. She managed to wriggle slightly nearer. Her hands were tied behind her back so she was unable to put her arms round her and give her a proper cuddle.

Her head was throbbing viciously. The pain in her legs was almost unbearable. Everything was getting much better in the hospital. Here, she was neither kept under the best conditions nor was she being treated by medical staff. One thing she knew - she was too poorly to be lying on a cave floor.

Maisie tried to reciprocate by sliding backwards. She endeavoured to nuzzle up to Madge. Although she was a stranger, Maisie saw she was a kind lady.

Sammy and Danny managed to hold back the tears. If you looked closely, you see traces of damp on their eyelashes.

Slowly, they told Madge what had happened. How they went down the tunnel a couple of times. How they investigated one leg of the tunnel and then the other. They told how they called it the 'rabbit hole' and this was their friend's 'rabbit hole.' It was in a lean-to which was in his Aunt Mary's garden.

On hearing the name "Aunt Mary," Madge started.

"What's your friend's name?" asked Madge.

"Why, it's Andy," replied Sammy.

Madge looked very startled.

"Is Andy staying at The Myrtles?" asked Madge.

This time it was the children's turn to look amazed.

"Yes," the three replied.

On seeing their surprised faces, Madge went on to explain she was Andy's Mummy.

You could have heard a pin drop. The long pause seemed to last for ever. Everyone started talking at once.

"Stop, stop," Madge said laughingly. Very briefly, she told them how she had an accident in the street when she was knocked over by a car. She told how she was hospitalised. She explained how two white-gowned men removed her from the hospital and kidnapped her.

She went on to say how she remembered being in the ambulance and passing the turn-off towards Auntie Mary's house. The next thing she remembered was being very uncomfortably tied up in the cave. She had no recollection of the period between.

She assured them to some extent it was not too bad as she kept drifting off into sleep. She did not know whether that was as a result of the accident or whether they were doping her through the meals they gave her.

Madge was thrilled to hear some recent news of Andy. She lingered on every word as they told her all they knew about what Andy was doing whilst she was in hospital.

For a few minutes, they forgot the terrible predicament in which they found themselves.

Maisie interrupted the general chit chat of conversation, "how are we going to get out of here?" Her tears once more flowed down her grubby face.

"Don't cry," said Danny kindly, "we've to think of a plan of escape."

"Well," said Sammy, taking charge as usual, "it's no use going back the way we came in, even if we could get out of this cave that way. There's only one way to go out and that is to go out from here."

"How are we going to do that, ti, ti, tied up?" Maisie stuttered

"We'll have to get untied up," announced Sammy, in a grown up, matter of fact, sort of way.

He explained about this film he had seen where they all got back to back. They were able to untie each other.

No sooner said, and the four of them shuffled together, back to back.

It took about half an hour before Sammy was able to untie Madge. You could hear a lot of grunting and groaning as his usually nimble fingers stumbled over the very firmly tied knots. The real difficulty was he was unable to see what he was doing. Everything was done by feeling his way. This was very difficult, as his own hands were securely tied behind his back.

When Madge was free, everyone let out a low cheer.

Slowly, Madge rose to her feet. She felt very unsteady. She knew she had to make the effort. The pain in her legs made her wince. Hurriedly, she released the other three children.

They stood up. They waved their arms and legs about in order to refresh the circulation.

Sammy went on to explain more fully.

"In the film, they continued to pretend they were tied up so the baddies wouldn't know."

He had hardly spoken these words when there was a grating sound. The four prisoners dropped to the hard floor unceremoniously. They put their hands behind their backs and linked the ropes over them. They tried not to sound as if they were out of breath.

Four men entered the cave. They were chatting as they came in. They kept their voices very low so they could not be heard. However, they had not reckoned on Madge's exceedingly good hearing.

"The final shipment of machines will be here in three days," said the tall one. "When they're all assembled, the entire world will know what we've done."

A slightly smaller man, who Madge recognised as one of her captors, laughed menacingly.

"They sure will, Boss."

"These machines, here, are all ready now," continued the Boss. "Once the containers underneath each machine have the chemicals added to them from Braders, everyone will see machines bobbing all over the place."

Madge was stunned when they mentioned Mark's work place – Braders.

"All we need now is Mark Appleyard help us put it all together. It's a pity we couldn't get hold of that boy, Andy, whilst they were in France. I don't know where he disappeared to," The Boss added.

Madge's eyes opened wide with fear which quickly turned to hatred. So that was what Mark had been up to, that was why he was so horrid these last two years.

What was this about Andy? Was he missing in France? Her mind was in a whirl. Before she could think further the four of them walked over to Madge and the children.

They looked, without pity, at the heap of flesh huddled on the floor. Madge hurriedly closed her eyes. She pretended she was asleep.

"What do you want us to do with the children, Boss?" asked Joe.

"Let's kill them," said Mike. As he spoke he whipped out a shiny knife from out of his black leather jacket and menacingly thrust it towards the children.

"It will be my pleasure for today," he said with a blood curdling laugh.

The children looked up at him with absolute terror on their faces. This pleased Mike. He gave a sneering smile in response.

"No, no," said the Boss "not yet, they can be our first audience. They can be our guinea pigs."

He was pleased with the idea and would enjoy seeing them squirm.

Casually, he walked over to a machine which was set apart from the other machines. It was circular and very thin. It looked a bit like a pizza.

He carefully removed it from off the bench and walked back towards the children.

With an evil chuckle, he lifted it up, took aim, and beamed it at Madge and the children.

Suddenly, Madge and the children heard flies buzzing round their head, on top of their head, in their head. It sounded as if there were flies everywhere.

The sound continued endlessly. It was like a million blue-bottles in the throws of death. The sound increased louder and louder. Deafening them was an understatement.

It was very hard not to put their hands to their ears. Their hands were fidgeting behind their back. They tried to rise up, as if they had a mind of their own. With great determination, they held them down. They knew their captors must not know they were loose from their bonds.

The noise went on and on and on. It was if the flies tunnelled right down, deep into their ears. They seemed to be gnawing at and eating their very brain.

Madge and the children screamed with terror.

.

CHAPTER THIRTY

He would not tell them how he would acquire the documents. However, he was in a position to obtain the documents the District Attorney failed to disclose. His skills not only lay in acquiring the documents but identifying the correct papers.

Andy was pleased his Auntie Mary let him stay over night with his Dad. At least, he would not have to hold on to his pyjama bottoms this morning.

He dressed quickly and went down to breakfast: his thriller under his arm. He hoped Pete and Harry would prove their innocence.

At breakfast, his Dad talked about Madge. He explained how he understood how sad and worried they both were about her accident and now her disappearance.

"Andy, our worrying about Mum won't change things. Let's do something to cheer ourselves up," he said.

"Shouldn't we stay home in case someone rings?" asked Andy.

"I don't think it will make any difference. We've the mobile. In a car we soon can be where we're needed."

"I don't know. I'm so sad. I do miss Mum."

"Will going to Blackpool cheer us up?" Mark enquired.

"It might," said Andy still looking very downcast.

"Well, let's go and see if it helps. Finish your breakfast and go and get ready"

After finishing his breakfast, Andy waited for his Dad by the front door.

It was good to be home again and see all the familiar things round him. It was good to go out of the front door instead of keep going out of Auntie Mary's back door. The very first time he had seen it opened was when the Social Worker came round the other day.

As he and Mark walked down the path, Andy put on his goggles and multicoloured hat. He jumped into the white Mercedes. Soon they were purring down the motorway.

They headed north until just after the junction to Preston.

"Look Dad, there's the Blackpool turnoff onto the next motorway."

They zoomed along past open fields populated by sheep. Andy called out, "I've seen it first, I've seen it first, I can see the Tower. There's Blackpool Tower." The words rushed and tumbled one after the other.

Blackpool Tower is more than a hundred years old and built on the style of the Eiffel Tower in Paris. It is a distinctive landmark as you look over the flat fields of the Fylde area which surrounds Blackpool.

Soon they were on the last leg following the Blackpool South Shore signs.

When they reached the Promenade, Andy looked out to sea. He knew from his Geography teacher, there was only the Isle of Man and Ireland between Blackpool and America.

To Andy's right was Central Pier which jutted out into the sea and to his left was South Pier which did the same. In the distance he saw North Pier.

Much more exciting to Andy was the Pleasure Beach.

Mark was pleased to get a parking place in a crowded side street, alongside the Pleasure beach. They walked in by the main entrance.

"Dad, I want to go on everything," said Andy.

Mark laughed.

They went into the entrance. Mark paid for two wristbands and a free park map.

"Dad, look it says there are one hundred and twenty five rides and attractions to choose from. We'll have to be pretty smart to get round them all."

They set off into the Pleasure Beach proper. Andy was skipping along brimming full of excitement. His eyes grew round and large as he saw all the rides he could go on. He didn't know where to start.

Mark was pleased to see how his idea cheered up Andy. He had been trying to think of things which would take Andy's mind off his Mum.

Throughout the Pleasure Beach were individual stalls where you threw things and win prizes. Holiday makers walked past them carrying large teddy bears or huge dolls. These they won at one of these stalls. Quite a few people were eating large pink sticks of candy floss.

Andy was spoiled for choice. In the end, he settled for the dodgems. These varied coloured small cars had a long pole reaching to the roof of the canopy which connected the cars to the electricity supply. Andy was glad he was big enough to get in. It was great fun driving the cars and ramming into other cars.

Mark watched benevolently and with pleasure as he saw his son enjoying himself.

Momentarily, the worries and anxieties of his wife disappearing were diminished.

Hardly was the dodgem ride over, before Andy was rushing to another booth.

"Come on, Dad, let's go on the ghost train," shouted Andy.

They settled into one of the carriages of the train. It whizzed through tunnels at quite a fast speed. Andy and Mark sat side by side, in one of the front carriages.

Andy did not like to admit he was scared. The worst moment was when that cobwebby thing came down into his face. The whole train was a domino of screams. Andy added lustily to their chorus.

His legs were still shaking and his face was a few shades lighter when they emerged into the sunshine. He wondered if he was ready for the Big One.

Everyone at school talked about it. He could hear the others saying "Scardey scaredy custard," if he did not go on it.

With a smile which belied how he felt, Andy said, "come on, Dad, let's go on the Big One."

Mark was also apprehensive but he did not want Andy to know. He did not want Andy to go on the Big One by himself.

As they drew near, the undulating track seemed to touch the sky itself.

Andy was very disappointed to discover he was two centimetres too small to go on it.

"Never mind, Mark said. "Let's go on the Big Dipper. That's nearly as good.

They hurried over to the Big Dipper. They buckled themselves into their carriage, waited expectantly, and whoosh, they were off.

At first, the ride was gentle and tame. Andy wondered what all the fuss was about.

He looked round. His heart nearly failed him. In one of the carriages behind him were two men. One he recognised as the one he saw from the tunnel. The other was a stranger.

Even they were momentarily forgotten; when the roller coaster went swoosh down, swoosh up. Andy's tummy felt as if it had left his body. He had never been on a roller coaster like it in his life.

He wished he had not drunk the large glass of milk for his breakfast. One minute the milk was in his mouth and the next it flowed down again. He clung onto his Dad's trousers as if his life depended on it.

Which was worse? Going down? Or was it worse going up the next leg of the roller coaster.

They reached a very high peak. Andy blinked in amazement. It was if there were no track at all. He realised it was almost a vertical drop to the ground. He closed his eyes and clung on for grim death.

Finally, they came to a halt. His legs hardly held him up. The ground was no longer solid, it felt spongy. It was like walking on soft rubber. Thankfully, he managed to keep the milk down.

He looked at his Dad who seemed unnaturally quiet.

Still, he would be able to boast to everyone at school he had been on the Big Dipper.

A mischievous thought crossed his mind.

"Should we go on it again, Dad?" he cheekily asked.

"No," said his Dad, very firmly. "I think it's time you went on something like the horse roundabout, by yourself."

Andy was about to retort it was too tame, when he remembered the two men he saw on the Roller Coaster.

He looked round. He saw them slightly obscured by the Laughing Clown booth. The Laughing Clown was chortling away. He was surrounded by a group of people laughing their heads off with him.

"Dad," Andy said nervously, "you won't believe it, I think those two men are following us."

"Don't be silly, Andy, you've been watching too much television."

"No, Dad." He thought for a moment whether he should tell his Dad about the tunnel and decided against it.

"One of them was on our plane to Nice. I saw him again whilst we were in Nice. He was with this other man in a few carriages behind us on the Big Dipper and now they're by the Laughing Clown."

Mark was about to say again to Andy. "Don't be silly," when he caught a glimpse of a gun pointed at him.

"Quick, Andy," Mark commanded, "run, run side to side. Run like mad to the car."

As soon as the two men saw Mark and Andy run they gave chase. This was difficult because of the group round the Laughing Clown.

A shot rang out above the laughter. The crowd fell to the floor as if as one man.

"Weave in and out," shouted out Mark again. Andy knew what his Dad meant, as he had seen people do it in films on the television.

Together, they ran through the Pleasure Beach. Rides and stalls which had seemed so attractive minutes before were just a blur.

At the precise moment, a man in one of the booths shouted out, "throw a coconut to win a big teddy bear," Andy heard the second shot which came from in front of him.

As he skidded to a halt, he realised it was a rifle range.

Suddenly, another shot came from behind. Andy felt the bullet whiz past his ear. He looked at his Dad's face. He saw fear in his eyes. Their white Mercedes was in view. Would they make it?

.

CHAPTER THIRTY ONE

It was difficult entering the District Attorney's office but Charlie knew where to look and how to find the right documents. He rifled through the papers and extracted what he wanted and slipped out into the night.

"Hi Norma," said Julie, "what's up?"

"I'm having trouble with this Appleyard case. I don't know where I'm going with it."

Norma told Julie about the various people she contacted. She approached Andy's school where he was doing well. She rang the Doctor and there were no problems there. Finally, she contacted the Police. As expected there were no problems there. She read the Court documents.

She told of her home visit to see Mark and Andy Appleyard. She was pleased how well it went. She was comforted with how well Andy related with his Dad.

"I agree with you, things don't add up. If Mother Madge is to be believed, Mark is a man who is violent and becoming increasingly so. You should have serious concerns about Andy being with him for any length of time. If what you saw at the home and Andy's relationship with his Dad is to be believed that paints a very different picture."

"Yes," said Norma," you've summed it up very well. Another thing troubles me. This disappearance, everybody is saying Madge has been kidnapped. What if she's done a disappearing act herself?"

"Wouldn't the hospital CCTV footage show what happened?" asked Julie.

"Yes, I agree. It shows Madge being taken out on a wheelchair," replied Norma, "but Madge could have got a friend to help her. Nothing adds up." She knew she was making huge assumptions but once started on this line she knew she had to go on.

She paused for a breath, as if she did not dare voice her next suspicion, "and what if," she continued, "the road traffic accident wasn't an accident at all, but was a suicide attempt by Madge?" Norma let out a sigh of relief as if all the pent up concerns were now shared.

"Then," answered Julie, "It's clear Madge has a very serious problem. She desperately needs help. If Andy continues to live with her, she may well need a package of support from various experts such as a psychiatrist.

"I had a case a little bit like that some time ago. The experts called it Munchausen's Syndrome," continued Julie. "The wife accused the husband of tying the children up and locking them in the coal shed. The children were only age three and four so it was difficult to work out the truth of the matter. The wife complained the children were very ill. She kept taking them to the hospital with a high temperature."

"How did you realise there was a problem with the wife: she was lying?" asked Norma.

"The hospital staff became suspicious of all the visits. They were even more suspicious when the children became worse after their Mother visited them. The hospital contacted the Social Services.

Together the hospital and Social Services evolved a plan whereby they installed surveillance cameras which showed what happened when the Mother visited."

"So what was the Mother doing?" asked Norma.

"The Mother was a trained nurse. When they were in hospital, the cameras showed her clearly giving the children injections. The contents were found to be a mild poison. It was sufficient to give the children a high fever.

The hospital challenged her but she denied the problem. When they required her to look at the video evidence, she collapsed in a heap of tears. I'm not sure she even realised she had a problem."

"She was certainly very dangerous," said Norma.

"Yes," replied Julie, "the children went to live with their Father. The Mother saw the children once a week at a Contact Centre where there was fairly close supervision."

"But that," continued Julie with a wry smile, "doesn't help you."

Norma was about to reply when the telephone rang. Julie leaned forward and picked up the phone.

"The call is for you, Norma, it's your friend, Terry. He says he's some information about Braders, the chemical firm."

Norma was waiting impatiently for this call for a few days. She was delighted to hear from Terry. They had a short conversation on the phone. She did not enlighten him as to her problem. She arranged to meet him at a local café in the high street at 7pm.

The time passed quickly as Norma worked on her paperwork. At quarter past six she hurried from work, leaving a selection of papers on her desk. She was always early for her appointments.

She entered the café where the proprietor greeted her warmly. She was a regular visitor to this café after work. She sat down and waited and waited.

Norma drummed her fingers on the table in the café. She had been here some thirty minutes. How much longer had she to wait for Terry?

"It was just like him," she thought to herself. She kept promising herself to buy him a watch. She could have kicked herself on arriving so early. She realised when they agreed a time that was the time he left wherever he was.

It was a terrible day for her. She had a huge report to finish which needed to be in Court by ten the following morning. It took her weeks to prepare. A few more hours were still needed on it. Gone was her lazy evening. She would be up until Midnight.

In addition to getting the Report to the Court, she had to give evidence in another long running saga. This would take a couple of hours of her day. This latter case had been going on for about five years.

The Mother repeatedly agreed Court orders. These allowed the children's Grandparents to take out the two children. When the day came for them to go out with their Grandparents, the Mother said they were ill or they had to go to a party or any excuse which prevented the Grandparents seeing the children.

This was a real dilemma to Norma. When she saw the children with their Grandparents, there was lots of fun and laughter. She saw the children loved being with their Grandparents.

Prior to the parents separating, the children called in at their Gran's every day, on their way home from school.

Their Gran gave them their tea of sandwiches and cakes. Their Mum picked them up and took them home.

When the Mother was working late, the Grandparents took them swimming. At the week-end the children stayed overnight so their Mum and Dad could go out.

Sadly, as soon as the parents separated, the Mum prevented the children seeing her husband's parents. They rang and the Mum put the phone down. They wrote but never heard from the children.

The Grandparents were at their wits end. They desperately wanted to know how their grandchildren, Jenny and Jane, were getting on.

Thus, they resorted to the Court. They used their life savings as it cost them thousands. Their Barrister worked hard on their behalf and they were delighted with the result. All the money spent was worth it to see their grandchildren.

Their rejoicing at getting the Court Order they wanted was soon quelled when they discovered the Mother had no intention of allowing them see the children.

Norma was deep in thought about trying to think of ways to help the Mother understand it was good for the children to see their grandparents.

Perhaps, she could try obtaining some counselling for the Mother.

The Mother had some counselling at the beginning of the case. She stopped it prematurely saying it was no good. Norma did not hold out much hope the Mother would be willing to start it again.

Norma was running out of ideas how to move this case forward so the children had the benefit of seeing their loving grandparents.

As Madge mused upon these matters, she heard a warm, deep voice boom out.

"Is anybody in?" Norma looked up. She saw a tall, bronzed man. He had dark wavy hair and brown deep set eyes which seemed to have a permanent twinkle in them.

"Sorry," she said with a smile, "I was thinking of tomorrow's case. Come and sit down."

Norma proceeded to order coffee and muffins.

"I'm glad you could make it. I was really pleased to receive your telephone call, Terry," she said, "I've been troubled by a case I'm on at the moment. I can't give you the names because it's privileged information. I thought you could give me some help."

"How can I help?" queried Terry, "I'm not trained in sorting peoples problems out, I'm a chemist."

"That's just it. I need the help of a chemist. More particularly, I need information about Braders."

She filled in some of the background of the case. The mystery the Father had only become violent since working at Braders,

She thought she better not complicate the matter by telling of her theory about the Mother.

"So you see, Terry, I find it quite bewildering." Norma said with some exasperation in her voice.

"Well," said Terry thoughtfully, "there are two possible explanations. One is the stress of the work was getting him down, particularly with all the travelling he was doing. Or it may be the chemicals he handled had an adverse effect on him. Let me do some investigation and get back to you."

He paused and leant back in his chair. A look on his face suggested he was not sure whether to share something.

"There's some unusual talk about what is going on at Braders. Perhaps my investigations will help," he mysteriously added.

CHAPTER THIRTY TWO

Charlie met up with Pete and Harry at the pre-arranged place and triumphantly handed over the vital documents. They paid him the balance of the fee they agreed.

The Boss looked malevolently at their curled up figures on the floor. Their faces scrunched up in anguish. Their faces contorted in agony. He wondered how long they could stand the buzzing sound.

He had done a number of experiments on animals. He started with mice. This was followed by taking a team of men to Africa to conduct some experiments on higher mammals such as chimpanzees. All this experimentation was done secretly and stealthily. He had to keep it secret from the authorities.

The initial testing was fairly easy to conceal as he learned what the safe level of the blast of sound was. He knew the laser torch was used for recreational purposes. It gave people a wonderful experience as they listened to music. Everyone believed he was creating panoply of musical sound for their enjoyment.

215

Later, they were more furtive in their experimentation as they gradually increased the level of sound.

It was increasingly difficult to handle the animals. They became distraught and dangerous. They abandoned working with the animals.

They guessed at the possible outcome of the last stage of the research. What impact the sound would have on humans.

Using the non linearity of the air, the ultrasound wave was guided by the red laser beam which projected from the centre of the wafer thin and lightweight black transducer. This produced a point of sound which was totally under the control of the one operating the machine. The transducer was about ½ inch thick and one foot in diameter: large pizza shape and size.

It enabled the Boss to pin point where he wanted the sound to go. The sound travelled down the very narrow beam of ultrasound. The wonderful part was he beamed the sound at one person and another person would not be able to hear it. This was its power. Sound was blasted at one individual and those around would not hear it.

Madge and the children were the first people to receive a blast beyond the comfortable level. The Boss was very pleased with the result.

A weapon in his hands: an instrument which gave him power. A device he believed would give him full autonomy over the world. The only dream in his heart was to rule the world. Make people do what he said.

The Boss switched off his laser sound torch and laughed in a menacing way, "that's just the beginning," he sneered.

As soon as he switched off the laser sound, the awful buzzing noise stopped.

He unfolded his cunning plan. As Madge listened shivers went up and down her spine and she realised how dangerous these men were. They were real terrorists. In fact they were worse than terrorists as they were totally mad.

She and the children had the foresight to retain their gags on their mouths. This to some extent muffled their screams. It was as well Madge had a gag on her mouth. Otherwise, she would have told the men what she thought of them. She imagined what her sister Mary would say. Auntie Mary would have wiped the floor with them without any thought of the consequences.

The Boss was very proud of his ideas. He was willing to share them to this captive audience. Bit by bit the plan emerged.

The machines were unique as they were anti-gravity machines. The small container at the base of each machine was to hold the chemicals from Braders chemical factory. These chemicals and the 'bubble-like head' of the machine would enable the machines to fly. Well, that was not quite true. They were not going to fly, as such, but levitate against gravity.

The Boss knew little of the work famous scientists had done on the subject of gravity. Men like Galileo, Kepler, Isaac Newton and, more recently, Albert Einstein. Although gravity was regarded as a weak force in science, none of these men discovered a way to defeat gravity. But the Boss thought he was cleverer than any scientists!

Whilst on holiday in Poland, the Boss met a Russian. The Russian told him of these wonderful flying machines which cost very little to run. He told him of the supersonic laser sound machines. He told him he would rule the world if he acquired them. Oh, what a lot he told him. The Boss lapped it all up. He knew he must have these machines whatever it cost.

The Russian took him back to Russia. He introduced him to a similar minded group of people. They knew they could never develop the idea in Russia without the authorities discovering what they were doing.

Thus it was, they were prepared to sell their ideas and the formula to the Boss for a modest sum. They made some money. At the same time, their ideals would be promulgated more widely. They all knew the synergetic power of the brotherhood of terrorists.

They told him where he could acquire the individual parts. They directed him to suitable carriers to ship the parts to the United Kingdom.

It took a little while to contact the various sources.

Whilst the Boss was waiting for the shipments to arrive, he made detailed preparation. Everything he did was precise and thorough. He assembled a group of willing workers whom he knew he trusted. These were people with the same ideology as himself.

He organised the excavating of the two tunnels with a cover factory at each end. A factory which hid the true nature of what he was doing.

This was easier than he expected as he had found these disused quarry tunnels.

In the factories, they assembled vacuum cleaners for distribution. The real work was the assembly of the anti-gravity machines in the cave.

He had two tunnels. If ever there were a problem one could operate as a decoy for the other. It would also act as a means of getaway in an emergency.

Once the hardware was assembled, it was a case of mixing the chemicals in the right amounts.

These were very small machines. They were relatively low weight. Each terrorist would wear the machine on his back like a satchel and fly without calling into any airports.

Because they were anti-gravity machines, the cost of using the machines was very little. They would travel for thousands of miles without the need for refuelling. The chemicals seemed to last for ever once they had given the initial thrust. This was the real beauty of these machines.

On arrival at the targeted city, they would take the machines from off their backs. The really clever part was that the machines could fly themselves. They would be directed by remote controls.

The terrorists would attach the laser sound machine to each anti-gravity machine and direct them into the most populous of areas.

As people looked up, on seeing the machines, they would be met with a blast of sound which would cause them much distress. In the end, their hearts would fail them. The people would die.

As Madge listened to these evil plans, she recollected a story she heard in School. How Joshua won the battle of Jericho. He and his entire army marched round the city once a day for six days with trumpets blowing. On the seventh day, they marched round the city seven times. On this final day, the seven trumpets, made out of ram's horns, were blown with a single blast. The people gave a mighty shout. The sound caused the walls of Jericho to fall down.

She knew already the power of sound. To use it directly on people was a most malicious and devilish plan.

The Boss told how they could recall the machines. The terrorists would put them onto their backs and fly safely away.

As the Boss was explaining his plan, Joe and Mike had gigantic, sickly grins on their faces.

"If accidentally, we get into the line of fire, we won't hear anything, as we'll be safe-guarded," he continued with a low laugh. "The people don't even know ordinary ear plugs would protect them."

"Oh, yes," he said exultantly, "I'll rule the world."

As Madge looked at the megalomaniac in front of her, she knew what a terrible event it would be. The few seconds they suffered was like a life time. She still heard the echo of the buzzing sound in her ears, even though the laser was switched off

What could she do about it? Even if they rushed the men, they would soon be over powered.

It was at times like this Madge wished she had taken Andy advice to carry a mobile phone. She realised what a silly thought that was. It is unlikely she would have had it tucked into her nightdress when she was kidnapped.

Even if she had a mobile phone she could not use it in front of them! Her mind did have silly thoughts sometimes.

She looked at the children. She saw their eyes were open wide with fear. They looked scared stiff. In turn, they saw the terror in Madge's eyes. She wondered how they would ever get out. Who could stop these depraved men in their iniquitous plans? Even if their anti-gravity ideas were far-fetched they could do a lot of damage with their sound machines.

The Boss strutted about somewhat agitated.

"What's up, Boss?" asked Mike.

"The other two should have been here by now with Mark Appleyard," he replied.

"The whole plan rests on his shoulders. Without his expertise in chemical mixing, we can't get these machines off the ground."

When Madge heard Mark's name mentioned, she felt sick in the pit of her stomach. To think they had been married all these years and she did not know he was involved in terrorist activity.

.

CHAPTER THIRTY THREE

Pete and Harry allowed themselves to be caught and taken to the Court. They listened incredibly as the District Attorney misled the Court.

Thankfully, the roof of the Mercedes was down. Andy and Mark threw themselves into the car. Mark started the engine which purred into life. He sped down the road. "It's a good job I've this new car," Mark thought.

The villains leaped into their vehicle. They hit the road in hot pursuit after them.

A madcap chase through Blackpool ensued.

Mark set off down the Promenade towards Lytham St Annes hoping to shake off his pursuers. Pedestrians jumped out of the way and stared open mouthed as the cars whizzed down the Promenade.

The villains were in very close pursuit. Mark was worried there would be a nasty collision by the more open spaces of the Sand Dunes.

At Squires Gate, he manoeuvred round the traffic signals. He treated the signals more like a roundabout and doubled back towards Blackpool.

After the Pleasure Beach, he turned inland. He weaved down the back streets until he reached the Town Centre. Here, he thought, he might have more chance of eluding his pursuers, but to no avail. They were close on his tail,

He decided to leave the precincts of Blackpool. He hoped his powerful car would shake them off.

First, they zoomed along Park Road: an arterial road in Blackpool. They sped along the wide dual carriageway of Preston New Road.

As they approached a large roundabout, Mark ignored the Motorway entrance. He thought the country route would give him more options if he got into difficulties.

The two men zigzagged in and out of other cars with careless indifference to their safety. Motorists gasped with astonishment. From time to time, a shot rang out as the two men tried to puncture the tyres on Mark's car.

They reached the boundaries of Preston. Mark turned into the old dock area. He weaved in and out past the supermarkets and office blocks.

Soon, they were out onto the country roads towards Auntie Mary's. All the time, they were closely followed by the two men.

Mark seized the opportunity, a few miles from Auntie Mary's, to pull into a side lane. The villains went whizzing past. They returned looking for Mark. At a fast speed, they flew past where Mark was waiting. Further down the road they turned round. Again they shot past him. This enabled him to pull out and continue his journey. Thus, Mark managed to put some distance between the two cars.

He wondered what they would do when they arrived at Auntie Mary's. These men were so wicked they would easily break into her home and kill them all.

"I wish there was somewhere for us to hide at Auntie Mary's," Mark muttered to himself.

"I know somewhere, Dad," Andy said cautiously.

It was clear this was the moment to tell his Dad about the tunnel. He explained all about his new friends. How they explored the tunnel. He told his Dad how he first saw two evil-looking men at the end of the tunnel.

Mark was speechless as he listened. It all sounded very peculiar. At least, it would be somewhere to hide until the Police arrived.

When they arrived at Auntie Mary's, he slammed on his brakes. They shot out of the car. The two ran through the garden into the lean-to. Andy pulled back the tarpaulin. They lowered themselves into the tunnel. They swiftly pulled the lid behind them.

Once in the tunnel, Mark could have kicked himself. He should have rung the Police when they were above ground. They dare not go back now. He took out his mobile. He carefully dialled the Police: no response. It was as he suspected, the mobile phone was unable to work underground. There was no time to go back. The men would at Auntie Mary's any minute.

They trudged down the tunnel. It was challenging walking in the dark. They only had Mark's cigarette lighter which kept going out.

They came to the division of ways.

"Which direction now do we take now, Andy?" asked Mark.

"We went along the left tunnel last time. When we got to the end, I looked out. I saw two men and behind them seemed to be a factory," replied Andy.

"Mmm, "said Mark, "perhaps we should look and see where the right tunnel goes."

Mark appreciated this was a risky strategy. Similar to Danny, he realised men do not build tunnels which lead nowhere.

They discovered, like Maisie and the twins before them, the right tunnel ended in a blank wall.

Using his lighter, Mark looked round at the wall. He found the piece of metal sticking out of the floor. He pulled at it.

As the door opened, Mark took off his shoe. He placed it by the door to prevent it closing.

A gasp was heard from inside the room.

It is not possible to say who was the more overwhelmed: Mark and Andy or Madge, Maisie and the twins.

Mark looked round in amazement at the equipment in the cave. Some of which mirrored his own laboratory.

"Is there a way out of here?" he asked.

"Yes," replied Madge, "I don't think we should use it as there are some wicked men on the other side of the exit. They might come back in here anytime."

It was clear there was no time for full explanations.

"Quick, follow us," commanded Mark. He was worried about going back, but hoped by the time they arrived at Auntie Mary's home the men would have gone.

Madge's head was in a whirl. She thought Mark was a terrorist yet he was rescuing them.

She preferred to risk her life with Mark. Mark was unlikely to kill Andy and the children.

Hastily, Mark retrieved his shoe and the door closed behind them.

They ran along the tunnel as quickly as they could. They helped each other out at the other end. They tumbled out into the daylight with a deep sense of relief.

They pushed the door of the lean-to. They were out into the garden: freedom at last.

They came to an abrupt halt as they looked down the barrel of a gun. The man emerged from behind a large, old Sycamore tree, with a gun in his hand.

"Not so fast my lovelies," he snarled, "I have you now. Who should I shoot first? Is it women and children first?"

The other villain joined him. He also had a gun in his hand.

The two had a low-voiced discussion as to what to do with their captives.

The taller one wanted to kill them there and then. He was concerned they would have difficulty getting two grown ups and four children along the tunnel. As he spoke, he was waving his gun about to emphasise each point he was making.

The other man wanted to get them all back to the cave and discuss the matter with the Boss.

Although the others could only hear snippets of the conversation, it was obvious they were intent on preserving Mark's life.

Mark called out, "kill me, but let my wife and children go."

The two men laughed at that as if it were a huge joke.

After some discussion, the taller one won the argument. As he raised his gun and pointed it at the shaking forms in front of him, he heard a whirring sound above him.

Looking up, he saw a helicopter hovering overhead. A loud report rang out. The villain dropped his gun in pain and fell to the ground holding his injured leg.

A team of Police officers emerged from out of the bushes. They captured the other man. They handcuffed them before throwing them into the waiting Police van.

Behind the officers, standing there majestically, was Auntie Mary.

Mark was flabbergasted the Police were there, when he had not rung them on his mobile phone.

Mark turned to the Police Office.

"I'm at a complete loss as to how you're here in the nick of time."

"It was Auntie Mary who rang us. She saw you and your son running fast through the garden. She saw these two strangers draw up in a car and watched them search her garden," replied the Officer.

"Auntie Mary!" they all exclaimed.

Andy did an unheard of thing. He ran up to Auntie Mary and gave her a big hug, "I love you, Auntie Mary."

Auntie Mary was secretly very pleased. She tried not to show it. She enjoyed all the attention she was getting as a heroine. Zero to hero in one fell swoop!

The next minute, Madge crumpled into a heap on the ground in the garden. Everyone looked on with deep concern

Mark knelt down on the ground alongside her. He tenderly held her hand. His heart was overwhelmed with love for her.

Gradually, Madge came round from her fainting attack. She looked up into the warm, adoring eyes of Mark. His eyes were full of compassion and tenderness.

Mark affectionately assisted Madge to her feet. He put his arm round her and helped her into the house.

Everyone squashed into the living room. Auntie Mary bustled round giving everyone tea and her special sponge cake.

Madge sat very quietly, partly, because the ordeal had been too much for her and, partly, because she was pondering the situation.

She was thrilled to be free but she had a massive problem. She saw the loving, caring look in Mark's eyes yet what was Mark's place in all this? Why had he rescued them if he were a terrorist? Should she tell the Police, Mark was a terrorist?

CHAPTER THIRTY FOUR

Triumphantly the trial lawyer for Pete and Harry produced the undisclosed documents. He publicly shamed the District Attorney.

The telephone rang in Norma's office. It kept ringing incessantly. Eventually reception asked Julie to go to Norma's office. A quick knock on the door and she went in. "Oh dear," said Julie to herself as she faced an empty office. She ran round everywhere looking for Norma

Julie was breathless with running round the building searching for Norma.

After some time she found Norma in a corridor. She was on her way back to her office.

"Norma, Norma, drive to Mary Macton's straightaway. There's been a huge to-do. The Police, helicopters. They've found Madge Appleyard."

"Police? Helicopters? Is Andy alright? Is Madge alright? Asked Norma.

"Oh yes, everyone is alright but you need to get over there as quickly as possible."

Norma threw on her coat. She dashed down the stairs. She jumped into her homely Robina. The car had done some miles in its fifteen years.

She hurried out of town and sped through he countryside. She went as fast as she dare along the narrow country lanes.

Today, she had no time for the pretty pink dog rose intermingled in the hedges. No thought as to its fruit high vitamin C level.

No glance at the bright yellow dandelions which lined the roadway. Normally she would have noticed these which she referred to as miniature chrysanthemums.

She screeched to a halt outside Auntie Mary's.

She was astounded to see the amount of Police cars and Police men milling about.

She strode up to the front door. It was opened by a beaming Auntie Mary. Norma introduced herself. Auntie Mary warmly invited her in.

Norma glanced into one room. She saw Madge talking animatedly with Police Officers. Norma went and sat down alongside a vibrant Madge.

The Police Officers gave Norma a précis of what had happened. She shared with them all she had learned about Braders.

She went into the other living room where Mark and Andy were sitting. Their face lit up when they saw Norma.
"You won't believe it." They exclaimed in unison.

Gradually, the events were unfolded to her. Her face was a permanent picture of astonishment. She was absolutely flabbergasted as she heard the details. They emphasized the part Auntie Mary played in the rescue operation.

Suddenly, there was a rustle behind her. She turned and saw Madge rushing in: her face aglow.

Madge ran up to Mark and embraced him passionately. "How can you forgive me, how can you ever forgive me?" She exclaimed.

Mark was overwhelmed with a deep love for Madge.

He pulled her onto his knee. He cuddled and rocked her like a baby. Tears were pouring down both their faces.

As they cuddled and talked, Madge explained how the Police told her about Braders. What the chemicals were doing to Mark. They told her how Mark probably saved her life and the children's lives by his brave actions.

Love and tenderness flowed like a river between them. Their eyes were bright and shiny with the joy of their reconciliation. Time seemed to stand still as they gazed into each other's eyes. For a while, they forgot everyone around them, as the embraced and hugged each other with joy and delight.

Andy jumped up and down excitedly "does this mean you and Dad are coming home?"

"Of course, darling." Replied Madge.

"We've been down a dark, horrible tunnel the last two years. At last we've escaped and come out into the light." Said Mark.

Looking hard at his Dad, Andy said, with a huge beam on his face, "Wow, the pull is back."

CHAPTER THIRTY FIVE

The Judge was astounded when Pete and Harry produced the documents Charlie acquired for them. A not guilty verdict was entered. Pete and Harry were free. Their awful nightmare was over.

District Judge Henson had an awful hour. It was a long time since he was so exasperated. How could an Advocate spend so much time talking about nothing? The lawyer neither knew the law nor the correct procedure.

He repeatedly asked the Advocate to deal with the issue in hand but to no avail. If he had been in a Criminal Court everyone would see, visually, he was a "whitewig."

Although only just out of Pupillage, the Barrister acted as if he knew it all. He was pompous, arrogant and repeatedly failed to listen to the Judge. Surely, someone taught him listening to the Judge was almost the first rule of advocacy.

District Judge Henson wondered what his Pupil Master had done with him in the twelve months he was a Pupil. It made it even worse the Barrister came from his old Chambers.

He determined to have a word with his Pupil Master. Tell him about this young upstart who had not learned to research his cases thoroughly. He would tell him the three rules of being a good Barrister: preparation, preparation, preparation.

Now, he had to turn his attention to the Appleyard case. He read the Papers the night before with concern. He, like Norma, realised something did not add up. He read Norma's CAFCASS report which was written some weeks earlier.

He was most probably going to follow Norma's helpful recommendation: Andy continues to reside with his Mother, Mark has visiting contact only.

He would stop overnight contact at this stage until he knew more about the problem. He would ensure the case was brought back before him in about sixteen weeks time.

He would give an Occupation Order to Madge. Thus, she and Andy would to return to the home safely. Mark had enough money to rent somewhere else whilst the matter was further investigated.

These were his preliminary thoughts. He would wait till he heard the full evidence before he finally made up his mind.

Mark and Madge and their respective Barristers went through a security locked door. They walked down a dark corridor and filed into the Judge's Chambers.

As before, Mark and Madge sat together at the top end of the table. The Lawyers sat down the side of the table. This time the atmosphere between Mark and Madge was very different. They were certainly more relaxed. The dismissal of the Proceedings was a mere formality. They gave each other a loving, encouraging smile.

Their respective Barristers told them, the Judge would allow the case to go through on the nod. They would be out in five minutes.

The Lawyers arranged their papers on the desk in front of them. They made a careful note of the time of starting the Hearing.

"Yes, Miss Smith?" District Judge Henson said, somewhat sharply.

"I am pleased to tell you, Sir, the parties are reconciled. Thankfully, that is the end of the case," Sue said with great satisfaction.

Sue Smith could not believe her ears when the Judge said, "no."

"No," she echoed.

"I said no. This is a children's matter. You cannot end the case without my permission. I am not going to give it."

With unaccustomed chivalry, Harry Jones manfully came to Sue Smith's rescue.

"Sir," he said "what my Learned Friend has said is correct. The parties are reconciled. We do not need to continue with the case."

"I do not think either of you are listening to what I am saying," said District Judge Henson. "I have to give permission for the case to end. I am not giving it. I am not a rubber stamp. Now, Miss Smith, will you open the case in the conventional manner."

To say Sue Smith was caught by surprise was an understatement of the highest order. To be perfectly honest, once she read they were reconciled, she only gave a cursory glance at the papers the day before.

"What was the Judge playing at?" she asked herself.

"Well, Sir," she said, as she turned the pages of her brief in panic.

"Well, Sir."

"Yes, Miss Smith, I heard you the first time, do get on," said the Judge.

Again Harry Jones intervened to try and help.

"Since when were you called Miss Smith?" District Judge Henson asked sarcastically.

This interchange at least gave Sue time to look at the chronology.

"Well, Sir," she said for the third time. "I think, Sir, if you were to turn to the chronology you would see the background to the case."

"Miss Smith," said District Judge Henson "you will be pleased to know that at least I (and he emphasised the word I as he said it) have read the papers."

"I should not really be so horrid to them," thought District Judge Henson. He knew they were very able Advocates.

Trying to put away the annoyance he was still experiencing from the earlier case. The Judge patiently explained the two matters which troubled him: the violence in the case and the change in Mark Appleyard.

"Well, Sir," said Sue, as if a record on a turn-table "I confess I stopped Miss Brent from coming. She is at the end of a telephone. I think she has up to date information which will help. Would adjourn for a few minutes?"

The case was stood down for a while. Sue rang Norma. She explained the situation.

Norma hurried over to the nearby Court. On the one hand, she would rather have not gone. She had other pressing matters to attend to. On the other hand, she was pleased to go. It was a case which had a happy outcome.

Half an hour later everyone was back in Court.

"Now, Miss Brent," said District Judge Henson, "as the parties apparently have reconciled, I am being asked to end this case. I am troubled about certain matters. You may be able to help me."

He outlined what was worrying him.

As the Judge explained, Norma was relieved she enlisted Terry's help.

"It seems, Sir, the problem was Mark was working for Braders. The firm has been taking certain shortcuts. They did not keep the chemicals in a proper environment," Norma said.

"Have the Health and Safety Government people been informed?" asked the Judge.

"Yes, Sir, the combination of the chemicals and the excess travelling had an effect on Mark. They caused of the change in his behaviour in the last two years. Now Mark has changed his job the problem should not reoccur."

"I am delighted to hear that," said District Judge Henson. He allowed himself a slight smile.

Norma went on to tell the thunderstruck Judge of the events of the last few weeks. She told him of Madge's suspicion Mark was a Terrorist. She recounted how when the Police Officer interviewed the two captured men, the full plan had emerged.

The villains tailed Mark for some time. They needed to get an idea of his routine and his habits. They believed Mark had the expertise and know-how to mix the correct chemicals in the right proportions to enable their anti-gravity machines take to the air.

They kidnapped Madge, as a hostage, to make Mark do what they wanted.

They intended to kidnap Andy, as well, but were thwarted. They knew he would do anything for his wife and child. It was their intention to forcibly apprehended him and bring him to the Cave.

For the first time in his career, Judge Henson was speechless. He never considered his job as a Judge to be very exciting. All he heard today changed his opinion. The exasperation of the earlier morning faded away.

"So, Miss Smith, you want my permission for you to end this case? You have my permission," said the Judge trying to sound nonchalant.

He turned to Madge and Mark. "May I wish you both all the best for the future? Remember Andy's welfare must always come first."

He paused for a moment. With a twinkle in his eye added.

"Please thank Auntie Mary for me."

"Yes, Sir," they chorused.

They left the Judge's Chamber and went into the large waiting room. They all gathered round in a circle as they gave their thanks to their Lawyers and to Norma.

Everyone left the building together.

Mark and Madge paused momentarily outside the Court's precincts.

As Norma looked back, she saw Mark give Madge a huge hug. She heard him say somewhat mischievously, "come, let's rescue Andy from Auntie Mary."

Hand in hand they walked across to where Andy and Auntie Mary were chatting, ten to the dozen, as they waited patiently in Mark's white sports car.

.

POSTSCRIPT

Two more villains in prison, a factory closed down and the tunnels sealed up. Yes, some escaped, but the Police would be relentless in their pursuit of the Boss and the other villains to ensure they did not start up their dastardly deeds again.

.

OTHER PRODUCTS

Look at www.pesha.com for other Pesha products such as:-

"Access to Children Course" on DVD by Pesha (Pat Bailey) who spent most of her forty years at the Bar working in the Family Court as an Advocate. She shares with you what she has learned in a four volume integrated course. The DVD volumes of the Course are interlinked so it is helpful to buy all the volumes and watch them in order.

This Course is about you and your children or grandchildren and gives ideas and information to help you see them and keep in touch.

"Being with your children or grandchildren brings a deep contentment which compares with no other experience. It is my heartfelt desire this Access to Children Course will enable you to enjoy this contentment once again,"

You will be surprised how easy it is to follow this Access to Children Course which is packed full of tips, secrets and strategies which hopefully will help you in your struggle to get access to your children or grandchildren. The Access to Children Course is in four volumes each volume of about an hour.

After sharing only one of her tips at a Grandparent's meeting more than twenty five percent reported success at the next meeting.

You will learn the best ways to get access to your children: possibly without a lawyer or going to Court. If you have go to Court you will learn what to do if you haven't a lawyer. If you have a lawyer you will learn how to make the best use of your lawyer and their costly time. You will learn how to make the best use of the Court.

You will discover getting access to your children usually has very little to do with the law. This makes the Access to Children Course internationally useful.

"My experience has been as an Advocate both in the Family Court and in high profile fraud cases and judging Employment cases. I have a law degree and postgraduate qualifications. I was Head of a Barristers Chambers for nine years. But none of this will compare to the achievement of helping you gain access to your children and grandchildren." Pesha

Bringing out her first DVD album **"Hymns of Heaven and Comfort" Album One** at seventy and with an MRI scan saying "highly suspicious of endometrial cancer," Pesha has Heaven and Comfort firmly in her mind. Thoughtfully and deeply heartfelt she shares these lovely old fashioned hymns with you. She hopes they will bring encouragement and comfort. Videos accompany Pesha's sensitive singing and words on screen enable you to sing along. There is a CD and MP3 version.

"Adventures of a Rebel" is an autobiography of Pesha's Father, Captain Robert Bailey. He was born at the beginning of the last Century in Bolton, Lancashire, England. There are five main sections. The first covers the Music Hall where his

Father was a professional comedian. The second covers his adventures with boats on the Thames and how he was shipwrecked off Foulness Island. The third is when he was conscripted during Second World War but volunteered to serve in the Indian Army and tells how he came to be on All India Radio. The fourth covers his caravanning adventures particularly in Spain. The fifth covers his dabbling as a property developer in Eire.

"Aroma of a Rebel." Sometimes the aroma is sweet, sometimes there's wholesome fun and sometimes there is a certain piquant. These poems are a lighthearted view of everyday life. Captain Robert Bailey wrote these poems whilst in his seventies. He commented on his daily life and what he read in the newspaper.

ABOUT PESHA

I hope you find my story inspirational.

I was first diagnosed with malignant cancer in 1988. The hospital said "oops our mistake we have re-run the biopsy of 1982 and it was malignant then."

After this diagnosis, operation and radiation, I would go and sit on the beach at Blackpool and think about the prospect of dying. As a Christian I knew where I was going but it is still an awesome thought as you contemplate a life cut short and the process of death.

I was very much inspired by a comment in an Edith Schaeffer book when it said "Life is too short not to take such risks which in our saner moments we would never consider."

When I was nearly fifty I started to take unimaginable risks such as the delight of fostering children.

In my early fifties I left my Barrister's Chambers in Manchester. Singlehanded, and on a shoestring, started a Barrister's Chambers in Preston to be nearer my foster children. I don't think there were many other Heads of Chambers who were lady Barristers. In fact when I was called to the Bar there were only just over a hundred lady Barristers in the whole of the country. I opened other business's some of which succeeded: other's have been a steep learning curve!!

Then in December 2008 I started to lose blood daily and in October 2009 the MRI scan said "highly suspicious of endometrial cancer." Many of my relatives had died of cancer including my Mother and Grandmother. Instead of going through the "I am going to die any minute syndrome," I made a major decision not to accept the treatment offered. I couldn't risk the loss of time and damage to my singing voice the side effects may cause as I had decided to create the "Hymns of Heaven and Comfort. Album One DVD."

One of the heartbreaks of our life is the effect on children when their parents separate. I remember my Mother picking me up from primary school when I was about nine. She asked me to go with her. She said "I'm leaving your Daddy." Even at that age I realized it was best to have both my parents. So I said "No." Why my Mother ever listened to me I will never know. But she stayed. Thankfully she had a most beautiful nature and was very loving and patient. Thus they stayed together for over fifty years until my Father died.

We were a family which was very much involved in the extended family. We would stay at Aunties and Uncles. We would often visit and they would visit us. This all seemed to bring a stability to life.

As a young Barrister I was thrust into the knowledge other families weren't like this. Siblings would fall out with each other and take each other to Court. Parents fell out and there were heated battles over who should have the children. This was all an alien world to me. I felt their pain and all I could do was fight their corner.

Quickly I realized these cases shouldn't be in the Court system. There were no winners but everyone lost. Most of all the children lost. The reason was everyone looked at their own pain and hurt. Through my own life's experiences I have discovered many of the principles I advocate in "Access to Children Course." I put them into practice. In other words they work in life as well as in Children Cases.

One of my joys in life is singing. As I couldn't afford studio fees I have had to learn to do everything myself.

I have learned a number of software packages.

Also I have learned to listen very carefully.

I hope it is a great encouragement to you that eventhough I am in my seventies I am bringing out my first DVD's and first novel. If I can do it you can too!

What is the secret? Just do it! Start and be persistent.

More details at
www.pesha.com